The Hollow Lands

Volume Two of a Trilogy
'The Dancers at the End of Time'

Michael Moorcock

Mayflower

Granada Publishing Limited
Published in 1975 by Mayflower Books Ltd
Frogmore, St Albans, Herts AL2 2NF

Made and printed in Great Britain by
Richard Clay (The Chaucer Press) Ltd
Bungay, Suffolk
Set in Linotype Baskerville

For Mike Harrison and
Diane Boardman

Let us go hence – the night is now at hand;
  The day is overworn, the birds all flown;
  And we have reaped the crops the gods have sown,
Despair and death; deep darkness o'er the land,
Broods like an owl; we cannot understand
  Laughter or tears, for we have only known
  Surpassing vanity: vain things alone
Have driven our perverse and aimless band.

Let us go hence, somewhither strange and cold,
  To Hollow Lands where just men and unjust
  Find end of labour, where's rest for the old,
Freedom to all from love and fear and lust.
Twine our torn hands! O pray the earth enfold
Our life-sick hearts and turn them into dust.

Ernest Dowson
A Last Word
1899

Contents

CHAPTER ONE

IN WHICH JHEREK CARNELIAN CONTINUES TO BE IN LOVE

'You have begun another fashion I fear, my dear.' The Iron Orchid slid the sable sheets down her smooth skin and pushed them from the bed with her slender feet.

'I am so proud of you. What mother would not be? You are a talented and tasty son!'

Jherek sighed from where he lay on the far side of the bed, his face all but hidden in the huge downy pile of pillows. He was pale. He was pensive.

'Thank you, brightest of blossoms, most revered of metals.'

His voice was small.

'But you still pine,' she said sympathetically, 'for your

Mrs Underwood.'

'Indeed.'

'Few could sustain such a passion so well. The world still awaits, eagerly, expectantly, the outcome. Will you go to her? Will she come to you?'

'She said that she would come to me,' Jherek Carnelian murmured. 'Or so I understood. You know how difficult it is sometimes to make sense of a time traveller's conversation, and I must say that it was particularly confusing in 1896.' He smiled. 'It was wonderful, however. I wish you could have seen it, Iron Orchid. The Coffee Stalls, the Gin Palaces, the Prisons and all the other monuments. And so many people! One might doubt a sufficiency of air to give life to them!'

'Yes, dear.' Her response was not as lively as it might have been, for she had heard all this more than once. 'But your re-creation is there, for all of us to enjoy. And others now follow where you led.'

Realizing that he was in danger of boring her, he sat up in his pillows, stretching his fingers out before him and contemplating the shimmering power rings which adorned them. Pursing his perfect lips he made an adjustment to the ring on the index finger of his right hand. A window appeared on the far side of the room and through the window sunshine came leaping, warm and bright.

'What a beautiful morning!' exclaimed the Iron Orchid, complimenting him. 'How do you plan to spend it?'

He shrugged. 'I had not considered the problem. Have you a suggestion?'

'Well, Jherek, since you are the one who has set the fashion for nostalgia, I thought you might like to come with me to one of the old rotted cities.'

'You are most certainly in a nostalgic mood, Queen of imaginative mothers.' He kissed her softly upon the lids of her ebony eyes. 'We were last there together when I was a child – you are thinking of Shanalorm, of course?'

'Shanalorm, or whatever it's called. You were conceived there, too, as I remember.' She yawned. 'The rotted cities are the only permanency in this world of ours.'

'Some would say they *were* the world.' Jherek smiled. 'But they do not have the charm of the Dawn Age metropoli, ancient as they are.'

'I find them romantic,' she said reminiscently. She threw jet arms around him, kissing him upon the lips with her mouth of midnight blue, her dress (living purple poppies) undulating and sighing. 'What shall you wear, to go adventuring? Are you still in a mood for those arrowed suits?'

'I think not.' (Privately, he was disappointed that she still favoured blacks and dark blues, for it indicated that she had not completely forgotten her relationship with doom-embracing Werther de Goethe.) He considered the problem for a moment and then, with a twist of a power ring, produced flowing robes of white spider-fur. His intention was to create a contrast, and it pleased her. 'Perfect,' she purred. 'Come, let's board your carriage and be off.'

They left his ranch (which was purposely preserved much as it had been when he had tried to prepare a home for his lost love, Mrs Amelia Underwood, before she had been projected back to her own 19th century) and crossed the well-tended lawns, where his deer and his buffalo no longer roamed, through the rockeries, rose bowers and Japanese gardens which reminded him so poignantly of Mrs Underwood, to his landau of milky jade. The landau was upholstered inside with the skins of apricot-coloured vynyls (beasts now long extinct) and trimmed with green gold.

The Iron Orchid settled herself in the carriage and Jherek seated himself opposite, tapping a rail as a signal for the carriage to ascend. Someone (not himself) had produced a lovely, round yellow sun and gorgeous blue clouds, while below them rolled gentle grassy hills, woods of pine and clover-trees, rivers of amber and silver, rich and restful to the eye. There was miles and miles of it. They headed in a roughly southerly direction, towards Shanalorm.

They crossed a viscous white and foamy sea from which pink creatures, not unlike gigantic earthworms, poked either their heads or their tails (or both), and they speculated on its creator.

'Unfortunately, it is probably Werther,' said the Iron Orchid. 'How he strives against an ordinary aesthetic! Is this another example of his Nature, do you think? It certainly seems primitive.'

They were glad to have the white sea behind them. Now they floated over high salt crags which glittered in the light of a reddish orb which was probably the real sun. There was a silence in this landscape which thrilled them both and they did not speak until it was passed.

'Nearly there,' said the Iron Orchid, peering over the side of the landau (actually she had absolutely no clear idea where they were and had no need to know, for Jherek had given the carriage clear instructions). Jherek smiled, delighting in his mother's enthusiasms. She always enjoyed their outings together.

Caught by a gust of air, his spider-fur draperies lifted around him, all but obscuring his view. He patted them down so that their whiteness spread across the seat and at that moment, for a reason he could not define, he thought of Mrs Underwood and his brow clouded. It had been much longer than he had expected. He was sure that she would have returned by now if she could. He knew that soon he must visit the ill-tempered old scientist, Brannart Morphail, and beg him for the use of another time machine. Morphail had claimed that Mrs Underwood, subject as anyone else to the Morphail Effect, would soon be ejected from 1896 and might wind up in any period of time covered by the past million years, but Jherek was sure that she would return to this Age. After all, they were in love. She had admitted, at long last, that she loved him. Jherek wondered if Brannart, determined to prove his theory flawless, were actually blocking Mrs Underwood's attempts to get to him. He knew that the suspicion was unfair, but it was already obvious that both My Lady Charlotina and Lord Jagged of Canaria were playing complicated games involving his and Mrs Underwood's fates. He had taken this in good part so far, but he was beginning to wonder if the joke were not beginning to pall.

The Iron Orchid had noticed his change of mood. She leaned across and stroked his forehead. 'Melancholy, again, my love?'

'Forgive me, finest of flowers.' With an effort he cleared his face of lines. He smiled. He was glad when, at that moment, he noticed violet light pulsing on the horizon. 'Shanalorm looms. See!'

As she turned, her face was a black mirror reflecting the delicate radiation. 'Ah, at last!'

They entered a landscape that none chose to change; not merely because it was so fine, but also because it might have been unwise to tamper with the sources of their power. Cities like Shanalorm had been built over the course of many centuries and they were very old. It had been said that they were capable of converting the energy of the entire cosmos, that the universe could be created afresh by means of their mysterious engines, but no one had ever dared to test this pronouncement. Though few had bothered to do so in the past couple of millennia (it was currently considered vulgar) it was certainly possible to make any number of new stars or planets. The cities would last as long as Time itself (which was not that long, if Yusharisp, the little alien who had gone into space with Lord Mongrove, was to be believed).

Beneath its canopy of violet light, which did not seem to penetrate to the city itself, Shanalorm lay dreaming. Some of its bizarre buildings had melted and remained in a semi-liquid state, their outlines still discernible; other buildings were festering – machine mould and energy-moss undulated across their shells, bright yellow-green, bile-blue and reddish-brown, groaning and whispering as it sought fresh seepages from the power-reservoirs; peculiar little animals, indigenous to the cities, scuttled in and out of openings which might have been doors and windows, through shadows of pale blue, scarlet and mauve, cast by nothing visible; they swam through pools of glittering gold and turquoise, feasting off half-metallic plants which in turn were nurtured by queer radiations and cryptically structured crystals. And all the while Shanalorm sang to itself, a thousand interweaving songs, hypnotic harmonies. Once, it was said, the whole city had been sentient, the most intelligent being in the universe, but now it was senile and even its memories were fragmented. Images flickered here and there among the rotting jewel-metal of the buildings; scenes of Shanalorm's glories, of its inhabitants, of its history. It had had many names before it was called Shanalorm.

'Isn't it pretty, Jherek!' cried the Iron Orchid. 'Where shall we have our picnic?'

Jherek stroked part of the landau's rail and the carriage began to spiral very slowly down until it was floating between the towers, skimming just above the roofs of blocks and domes and globes which shone with a thousand indefinable shades. 'There?' He indicated a pool of ruby-coloured liquid overhung with old trees, their long, rusted branches touching the surface. A soft, red-gold moss crept down to the bank and tiny, tinkling insects made sparkling trails of amber and amethyst through the air.

'Oh, yes! It's perfect!'

As he landed the carriage and she stepped daintily out, she raised a finger to her lips, staring around at the scene with an expression of faint recognition.

'Is this...? Could it be...? Jherek, you know, I believe this is where you were *conceived*, my egg. Your father and I were walking' – she pointed at a complex of low buildings on the opposite shore, just visible through a drifting, yellow mist – 'over there! When the conversation turned, as it will in such places, to the customs of the ancients. I think we were discussing the Dead Sciences. As it happened, he had been studying some old text on biological restructuring, and we wondered if it was still possible to create a child according to Dawn Age practices.' She laughed. 'The mistakes we made at first! But eventually we got the hang of it and here you are – a creature of quality, the product of skilled craftsmanship. Possibly that is why I cherish you so deeply, with such pride.'

Jherek took her hand of gleaming jet. He kissed the tips of her fingers. Gently, he stroked her back. He could say nothing, but his hands were gentle, his expression tender. He knew her well enough to know that she was strangely excited.

They lay down together on the comfortable moss, listening to the music of the city, watching the insects dancing in the predominantly violet light.

'It is the peace, I believe, that I treasure most,' murmured the Iron Orchid, moving her head luxuriously against his shoulder, 'the antique peace. Have we lost something, do you think, that our forefathers possessed, some quality of experience? Werther believes that we have.'

Jherek smiled. 'It is my understanding, most glorious of blooms, that individuals are given to individual experiences. We can make of the past anything we choose.'

'And of the future?' said she dreamily, inconsequently.

'If Yusharisp's warnings are to be taken seriously, then the future fades; there is scarcely any left.'

But he had lost her attention. She got up and walked to the edge of the pool. Below the surface warm colours writhed and, entranced for the moment, she stared at them. 'I should regret...' she began, then paused, shaking her dusky hair. 'Ah, the *smells*, Jherek. Are they not sublime?'

He raised himself to his feet and went to join her, a billowing cloud of white as he moved. He took a deep breath of the chemical atmosphere and his body glowed.

He looked across the pool at the outline of the city, wondering how it had changed since it had been populated by humankind, when people had lived their lives among its engines and its mills, before it had become self-sufficient, no longer needing tending. Did it ever suffer loneliness, he thought, or miss what must have seemed to it, at last, the clumsy, affectionate attentions of the engineers who had brought it to life? Had Shanalorm's inhabitants drifted away from the city, or had the city rejected them? He put an arm around his mother's shoulders, but he realized that it was himself shivering, touched for a moment by an inexplicable chill.

'They are sublime,' he said.

'Not dissimilar, I suppose, to the one you visited – to London?'

'It is a city,' he agreed, 'and they do not alter much in their essentials.' And he felt another pang, so he laughed and said: 'What shall be the colours of our meal today?'

'Ice white and berry-blue,' she said. 'Those little snails with their azure shells – where are they from? And plums! What else? Aspirin in jelly?'

'Not today. I find it a trifle insipid. Shall we have a snow-fish of some sort?'

'Absolutely!' Removing her gown, she flicked it out over the moss and it became a silvery cloth. Together they arranged the food, seating themselves on opposite sides of the cloth.

But when it was ready Jherek did not feel hungry. To please his mother, he sampled some fish, a sip or two of mineral water, a morsel of heroin, and was glad when she herself became bored with the meal and suggested that they disseminate it. No matter how much he tried to give his whole heart to his mother's enthusiasm, he found that he still could not purge himself of a vague feeling of unease. He knew that he would like to be elsewhere but knew, too, that there was nowhere in the world he could go and be rid of his sense of dissatisfaction. He noticed that she was smiling.

'Jherek! You sag, my dear! You mope! Perhaps the time has come to forget your rôle – to give it up in favour of one which can be better realized?'

'I cannot forget Mrs Underwood.'

'I admire your resolution. I have told you so already. I merely remind you, from my own knowledge of the classics, that passion, like a perfect rose, must finally fade. Perhaps it is time to begin fading a little?'

'Never.'

She shrugged. 'It is your drama and you must be faithful to it, of course. I would be the first to question the wisdom of veering from the original conception. Your taste, your tone, your touch – they are exquisite. I shall argue no further.'

'It appears to go beyond taste,' said Jherek, picking at a piece of bark and making it thrum gently against the bole of the tree. 'It is difficult to explain.'

'What truly important work of art is not?'

He nodded. 'You are right, Iron Orchid. That is all it is.'

'It will soon resolve itself, fruit of my seed.' She linked her arm in his. 'Come, let us walk for a while through these tranquil streets. You might find inspiration here.'

He allowed her to lead him across the pool while she, still in a mood of fond reminiscence, talked of his father's love of this particular city and the profound knowledge he had had of its history.

'And you never knew who my father was?'

'No. Wasn't it delicious? He remained in disguise throughout. We were in love for weeks!'

'No clues?'

'Oh, well...' She laughed lightly. 'It would have spoiled it to have pursued the secret too fiercely, you know.'

Beneath their feet some buried transformer sighed and made the ground tremble.

CHAPTER TWO

PLAYING AT SHIPS

'I sometimes wonder,' said the Iron Orchid as Jherek's landau carried them away from Shanalorm, 'where all the current craze for Dawn Age discoveries is leading.'

'Leading, my life?'

'Artistically, I mean. Soon, largely because of the fashion you began, we shall have re-created that age down to the finest details. It will be like inhabiting the 19th century.'

'Yes, metallic magnificence?' He was polite but still unable to follow her drift.

'I mean, are we not in danger of taking Realism too far, Jherek? One's own imagination can become clogged, after all. It was always your argument that travelling into the past rather spoiled one's conception – made the outlines fuzzy, as it were – inhibited creativity.'

'Perhaps,' he agreed. 'But I am not sure my "London" is harmed from being inspired by experience rather than fantasy. The fad could go too far, of course. In the case, for instance, of the Duke of Queens...'

'I know you rarely favour his work. It can be extravagant sometimes, a little, I suppose, empty, but ...'

'It is his tendency to vulgarize which disturbs me, to pile effect upon effect. I think he showed restraint in his "New York, 1930", for all the obvious influence of my own piece. Such influences might be good for him.'

'He, among others, could take it too far,' she said. 'That is what I meant.' Then she shrugged. 'But soon you'll set a fresh fashion, Jherek, and they will follow that.' She spoke almost wistfully, almost hopefully. 'You will guide them away from excess.'

'You are kind.'

'Oh, more!' Her raven face lit with humour. 'I am biased, my dear! You are my son!'

'I heard that the Duke of Queens had completed his "New York". Shall we go to see it?'

'Why not? And let us hope he'll be there, too. I am very fond of the Duke of Queens.'

'As am I, for all that I do not share his tastes.'

'He shares yours. You should be more generous.'

They laughed.

The Duke of Queens was delighted to see them. He stood some distance away from his design, admiring it with unashamed pleasure. He was dressed in a style of the 800th century, all crystal spirals and curlicues, beast eyes and paper bosses, with gauntlets which made his hands invisible. His sensitive face with its heavy black beard turned upwards as he called to Jherek and his mother:

'Iron Orchid, in all your swarthy beauty! And Jherek! I give you full credit, my dear, for your original inspiration. Regard this as a tribute to your genius!'

Jherek warmed to the Duke of Queens, as always. His taste might not have been all it could be, but his generosity was unquestionable. He determined to praise the Duke's creation, no matter what he thought of it privately.

It was, in fact, a relatively moderate affair.

'It is from the same period as your "London", as you can see. Very true to the original, I think.'

The Iron Orchid's hand tightened momentarily on Jherek's arm as they descended from the landau, as if to confirm the validity of her judgement.

'That tallest tower at the centre is the Empire State Apartments, in lapis lazuli and gold, built as the home of New York's greatest king (Kong the Mighty) who, as you know, ruled the city during its Golden Age. The bronze statue you see on the top of the building is Kong's...'

'He looks beautiful,' said the Iron Orchid, 'but almost inhuman.'

'It *was* the Dawn Age,' said the Duke. 'The building is just over a mile and a quarter high (I took the dimensions from an historical text-book) and a splendid example of the barbaric simplicity of typical architecture of the early Uranium Centuries – almost too early, some would say.'

Jherek wondered if the Duke of Queens were quoting whole from the text-book; his words had that ring to them.

'Are not the buildings crowded together rather?' said the Iron Orchid.

The Duke of Queens was not offended. 'Deliberately,' he told her. 'The epics of the time made constant references to the narrowness of the streets, forcing people to move crabwise – hence the distinctive "sidewalk" of New York.'

'And what are those?' said Jherek, pointing to a collection of picturesque thatched cottages. 'They seem untypical.'

'It is the village of Greenwich, a kind of museum frequented by sailors. A famous vessel was moored in the river. Can you see it?' He indicated something tied to a jetty, it glinted in the dark water of a lagoon.

'It appears to be a gigantic glass bottle,' said the Iron Orchid.

'So I thought, but somehow they managed to sail in them. Doubtless the secret of their locomotion has been lost, but I based the ship on a model of one I came across in a record. It is called the *Cutty Sark*.' The Duke of Queens permitted himself a smirk. 'And that, my dear Jherek, is where I have had the privilege of being imitated. My Lady Charlotina was so impressed that she has begun a reproduction of some other famous ship of the period.'

'I must say that your sense of detail is impressive,' Jherek complimented him. 'And have you populated the city?' He screwed up his eyes the better to see. 'Are those figures moving about in it?'

'They are! Eight million of them.'

'And what are those tiny flashes of light?' enquired the Iron Orchid.

'The muggers,' said the Duke of Queens. 'At that time New York attracted a good many artists, primarily photographers (called popularly "shooters", "muggers", or sometimes "mug-shotters") and what you see are their cameras in action.'

'You have a talent for thorough research,' said Jherek.

'I owe much to my sources, I admit,' agreed the Duke of Queens. 'And I found a time traveller in my menagerie who was able to help. He wasn't from exactly the same period, but close enough to have seen many records of the time. Most of the other buildings are in lurex and coloured perspex, favourite materials of Dawn Age craftsmen. The protective talismans are, of course, in neon, to ward off the forces of darkness.'

'Ah, yes,' said the Iron Orchid brightly. 'Gaf the Horse

in Tears had something similar in his "Canceropolis, 2215".'

'Really?' The Duke's tone was unintentionally distant. He was not fond of Gaf's work and had been known to describe it once as 'over-eager'. 'I must go to see it.'

'It's on the same theme as Argonheart Po's "Edible Birmingham, Undated", I believe,' said Jherek, to turn the subject a little. 'I tried it a day or two ago. It was delicious.'

'What he lacks in visual originality, he makes up for in culinary imagination.'

'Definitely a Birmingham of the mind,' agreed the Iron Orchid, 'and for the palate. Some of the buildings were blatant copies of My Lady Charlotina's "Rome, 1946".'

'A shame about the lions,' murmured the Duke of Queens sympathetically.

'They got out of control,' said the Iron Orchid. 'I warned her that they would. Not enough Christians. Still, I thought it drastic to disseminate it, merely because the population was eaten. But the flying elephants were lovely, weren't they?'

'I'd never seen a circus before,' said Jherek.

'I was just about to leave for Lake Billy the Kid, where some of the ships are being launched.' The Duke of Queens indicated his latest air car, a vast copy of one of the Martian flying machines which had attempted to destroy New York during the period in which he took an interest. 'Would you like to come?'

'A wonderful idea,' said the Iron Orchid and Jherek, thinking that one way of passing the time was as good as another, agreed.

'We shall follow in my landau,' he said.

The Duke of Queens gestured with one of his invisible hands. 'There is plenty of room in my air car, but just as you like.' He felt beneath his crystalline robes and produced a flying helmet and goggles. Donning them, he strode to his carriage, climbed with some difficulty up the smooth side and settled himself in the cock-pit.

Jherek watched in amusement as there came a roaring from the machine, a glow which was soon red-hot, a shower of sparks and a considerable amount of blue smoke, and then the contraption was lurching upwards. The Duke of Queens seemed to specialize in exceedingly unstable methods of transport.

Lake Billy the Kid had been enlarged for the occasion of the regatta (this, in itself, was unusual) and the surrounding mountains had all been moved back to accommodate the extra water. Small groups of people were gathered here and there on the shore, staring at the ships which had so far been presented. They made a fine collection.

Jherek and the Iron Orchid landed on the white ash of the beach and joined the Duke of Queens who was already talking to their hostess. My Lady Charlotina still wore several breasts and an extra pair of arms and her skin was a delicate blue; for decoration she had a collar from which trailed a few gauzy wisps of various colours. Her large eyes were alight with pleasure at seeing them.

'Iron Orchid, still in mourning I see. And Jherek Carnelian, most famous of metatemporal explorers. I had not expected you.'

Slightly put out, the Iron Orchid unostentatiously changed her skin colour to a more natural shade. Her gown became suddenly so blindingly white that they all blinked. She toned it down, murmuring apologies. 'Which of the boats is yours, dear?'

My Lady Charlotina pursed her lips in mock disapproval. '*Ships*, most venerable of plants. That one is mine.' She inclined her head in the direction of an immense reproduction of a woman, lying stomach-down in the water, her arms and legs spread out symmetrically, a crown of gold and diamonds upon her wooden head. 'The *Queen Elizabeth*.'

As they watched, a great gust of blackness billowed from the ears of the model and from the mouth (barely above the surface) there came a melancholy tooting.

'The one beside it is the *Monitor*, which carried off some virgins or something, did it not?' This was smaller than the *Queen Elizabeth*; the vessel's bulk representing a man's body, its back arched inwards, with a huge bull's head on its shoulders. 'O'Kala Incarnadine simply can't rid himself of his obsession with beasts. It's sweet, really.'

'Are they all of the same period?' asked the Duke of Queens. 'That one, for instance?' He pointed to a rather shapeless ship. 'It looks more like an island.'

'That's the S.S. *France*,' explained My Lady Charlotina. 'It's Grevol Lockspring's entry. The one just steaming towards it is the *Water Lily* – I'm sure it wasn't a real plant.' She named some of the other peculiarly wrought vessels. 'The *Mary Rose*. The *Hindenburg*. The *Patna*. And isn't that one beautiful – stately – The *Leningrad*?'

'They are all lovely,' said the Iron Orchid vaguely. 'What will they do when they are assembled?'

'Fight, of course,' said My Lady Charlotina in excitement. 'That's what they were built for, you see, in the Dawn Age. Imagine the scene – a heavy mist on the waters – two ships manoeuvring, each aware of the other, neither being able to find the other. It is, say, my *Queen Elizabeth* and Argonheart Po's *Nautilus* (I fear it will melt before the regatta is finished). The *Nautilus* sees the *Queen Elizabeth*, its foghorns disperse the mist, it focuses its funnels and – *whoosh!* – the *Queen Elizabeth* is struck by thousands of little belaying needles – she shudders and retaliates – from her forward ports (they must have been her breasts; that is where I've put them, at any rate) pour lethal tuxedos, wrapping themselves around the *Nautilus* and trying to drag it under. But the *Nautilus* is not so easily defeated ... Well, you can imagine the rest, and I will not spoil the actual regatta for you. Almost all the ships are here now. I believe there are a couple of entries to come, then we begin.'

'I cannot wait,' said Jherek absently. 'Is Brannart Morphail, by the by, still residing with you, My Lady Charlotina?'

'He has apartments at Below-the-Lake, yes. He is there now, I would guess. I asked him for help with the design of the *Queen Elizabeth,* but he was too busy.'

'Is he still angry with me?'

'Well, you did lose one of his favourite time machines.'

'It hasn't returned, then?'

'No. Are you expecting it?'

'I thought, perhaps, Mrs Underwood would use it to come back to us. You would tell me if she did?'

'You know that I would. Your relationship with her is my abiding interest.'

'Thank you. And have you seen Lord Jagged of Canaria recently?'

'He was supposed to come today. He half-promised to contribute a ship, but he is doubtless as lazy as ever and has forgotten. He might well be in one of those strange, unsociable moods of his. He retires, as you know, from society from time to time. Oh, Mistress Christia, what is this?'

The Everlasting Concubine fluttered long lashes over her wide, blue eyes. She was clad in filmy pink, with a pink hat perched on her golden hair. Her hands were dressed in pink gloves and she was presenting something which rested on her outstretched palms. 'It is not an entry, exactly,' she said, 'but I thought you might like it.'

'I do! What is it called?'

'The *Good Ship Venus.*' Mistress Christia smiled at Jherek. 'Hello, my dear. Does the flame of your lust burn as strongly as ever?'

'I am in love, these days,' he said.

'You draw a distinction.'

'I have been assured that there is one.' He kissed her upon her perfect nose. She tickled his ear.

'Where do you discover all these wonderful old emotions?' she asked. 'You must talk to Werther – he has the same interests, but does not pursue them with your panache, I am afraid. Has he told you about his "sin"?'

'I have not seen him since my return from 1896.'

My Lady Charlotina interrupted, placing a caressing hand upon Mistress Christia's thigh. 'Werther excelled himself – and so did you, Everlasting Concubine. Surely you aren't criticizing him?'

'How could I? I *must* tell you about Werther's "crime", Jherek. It all began on the day that I accidentally broke his rainbow...' And she embarked upon a story which Jherek found fascinating, not merely because it was really a very fine story, but also because it seemed to relate to some of the ideas he was himself mulling over. He wished that he found Werther better company, but every time he tried to have a conversation with the gloomy solitary, Werther would accuse him of being superficial or insensitive and the whole thing would descend into a series of puzzled questions on Jherek's part and recriminations on Werther's.

Mistress Christia and Jherek Carnelian strolled arm in arm along the shore while the Everlasting Concubine chatted merrily on. Out on Lake Billy the Kid the ships were beginning to take up their positions. The sun shone down on blue, placid water; from here and there came the murmur of animated conversation and Jherek found his good humour returning as Mistress Christia drew to the close of her tale.

'I hope Werther was grateful,' he said.

'He was. He *is* very sincere, Jherek, but in a different sort of way.'

'I need no convincing. Tell me, did he—?' And he broke off as he recognized a tall figure standing by the water's edge, deep in conversation with Argonheart Po (who was, as always, wearing his tall chef's cap). 'Excuse me, Mistress Christia. You will not think me rude if I speak to Lord Jagged?'

'You could never offend me, delicacy.'

'Lord Jagged!' called Jherek. 'How pleased I am to see you here.'

Handsome, weary, his long, pale face wearing just a shade of a smile, Lord Jagged turned. He wore scarlet silk, with one of his usual high, padded collars framing a head of shoulder-length near-white hair.

'Jherek, spice to my life! Argonheart Po was just giving me the recipe for his ship. He assures me that, contrary to the gossip, it cannot melt for at least another four hours. You will be as interested as I to hear how he accomplished the feat.'

'Good afternoon, Argonheart,' said Jherek with a nod to the fat and beaming inventor of, among other things, the savoury volcano. 'I was hoping, Lord Jagged, to have a word...'

Argonheart Po was already moving away, his hand held tightly by the ever tactful Mistress Christia.

'... about Mrs Underwood,' concluded Jherek.

'She is back?' Lord Jagged's aquiline features were expressionless.

'You know that she is not.'

Lord Jagged's smile broadened a fraction. 'You are beginning to credit me with prescience of some sort, Jherek. I am flattered, but I do not deserve the distinction.'

Disturbed because of this recent, subtle alteration in their old relationship, Jherek bowed his head. 'Forgive me, jaunty Jagged. I am full of assumptions. I am, in the words of the ancients, "over-excited".'

'Perhaps you have contracted one of those old diseases, my breath? The kind which could only be transmitted by word of mouth – which attacked the brain and made the brain attack the body...'

'Dawn Age science is your speciality, rather than mine, Lord Jagged. If you are making a considered diagnosis ...?'

Lord Jagged laughed one of his rare, hearty laughs and he flung his arm around his friend's shoulders.

'My luscious, loving larrikin, my golden goose, my grief, my prayer. You are healthy! I suspect that you are the only one of us that is!'

And, his usual, cryptic self, he refused to expand on this statement, drawing Jherek's attention, instead, to the regatta, which had begun at last. A vile yellow mist had been spread across the sparkling sea, making all murky; the sun had been dimmed, and great, shadowy shapes crept, honking, through the water.

Jagged arranged his collar about his face, but he kept his arm round Jherek's shoulders. 'They will fight to the death, I'm told.'

CHAPTER THREE

A PETITIONER AT THE COURT OF TIME

'What else is it but decadence,' said Li Pao, My Lady Charlotina's resident bore (and, like most time travellers, dreadfully literal-minded), 'when you spend your days in imitation of the past? And it is not as if you imitated the virtues of the past.' He brushed pettishly at his faded denim suit. He took off his denim cap and wiped his brow.

'Virtues?' murmured the Iron Orchid enquiringly. She had heard the word before.

'The best of the past. Its customs, its morals, its traditions, its standards ...'

'Flags?' said Gaf the Horse in Tears, looking up from

an inspection of his new penis.

'Li Pao's words are always so hard to translate,' said My Lady Charlotina, their hostess. They had repaired to her vast palace under the lake and she was serving them with rum and hard tack. Every ship had been sunk. 'You don't really mean flags, do you, dear?'

'Only in a manner of speaking,' said Li Pao, anxious not to lose his audience. 'If by flags we refer to loyalties, to causes, to a sense of purpose.'

Even Jherek Carnelian, an expert in Dawn Age philosophies, could scarcely keep up with him. When the Iron Orchid turned to him in appeal to explain, he could only shrug and smile.

'My point,' said Li Pao, raising his voice a fraction, 'is that you could use all this to some advantage. The alien, Yusharisp ...'

The Duke of Queens coughed in embarrassment.

'... had news of inescapable cataclysm. Or, at least, he thought it inescapable. There is a chance that you could save the universe with your scientific resources.'

'We don't really understand them any more, you see,' gently explained Mistress Christia, kneeling beside Gaf the Horse in Tears. 'It's a marvellous colour,' she said to Gaf.

'There are many here – prisoners of your whims, like myself – who, if given the opportunity, might learn the principles involved,' Li Pao went on, 'Jherek Carnelian, you are bent on rediscovering all the old virtues, surely you see my point?'

'Not really,' said Jherek. 'Why would you wish to save the universe? Is it not better to let it go its natural course?'

'There were mystics in my day,' said Li Pao, 'who considered it unwise to, as they put it, "tamper with nature". But if they had been listened to, you would not have the power you possess today.'

'We would still have been happy, doubtless,' O'Kala Incarnadine chewed patiently at his hard tack, his voice somewhat bleating in tone, owing to his having re-modelled his body into that of a sheep. 'One does not need power, surely, to be happy?'

'That was not exactly what I was trying to say.' Li Pao's lovely yellow skin had turned very slightly pink. 'You are immortal – yet you will still perish when the planet itself is destroyed. In perhaps two hundred years you will be dead. Do you want to die?'

My Lady Charlotina yawned. 'Most of us have died at some stage. Quite recently, Werther de Goethe hurled himself to his death on some rocks. Didn't you, Werther?'

Dark-visaged Werther sipped moodily at his rum. He gave a sigh of assent.

'But I speak of permanent death – without resurrection.' Li Pao sounded almost desperate. 'You must understand. None of you are unintelligent...'

'I am unintelligent,' said Mistress Christia, her pride wounded.

'So you say.' Li Pao dismissed her plea. 'Do you want to be dead for ever, Mistress Christia?'

'I have never considered the question that much. I suppose not. But it would make no difference, would it?'

'To what?'

'To me. If I were dead.'

Li Pao frowned.

'We would all be better off dead, useless eaters of the lotus that we are.' Werther de Goethe's jarring monotone came from the far side of the room. He glared down at his reflection in the floor.

'You speak only of postures, Werther,' the ex-member of the governing committee of the 27th century People's Republic admonished. 'Of poetic rôles. I speak of reality.'

'Is there nothing real about poetic rôles?' Lord Jagged of Canaria strolled across the room, admiring the flowers which grew from the ceiling. 'Was not your rôle ever poetic, Li Pao, when you were in your own time?'

'Poetic? Never. Idealistic, of course, but we were dealing with harsh facts.'

'There are many forms of poetry, I understand.'

'You are merely seeking to confuse my argument, Lord Jagged. I know you of old.'

'I thought I aimed at clarification. By metaphor, perhaps,' he admitted, 'and that does not always seem to clarify. Though it works very well for some.'

'I believe you deliberately oppose my arguments because you half-agree with them yourself.' Li Pao plainly felt he had scored a good point.

'I half-agree with *all* arguments, my dear!' Lord Jagged's smile seemed a touch weary. 'Everything is real. Or can be made real.'

'With the resources at your command, certainly.' Li Pao agreed.

'It is not exactly my meaning. You made your dream real, did you not? Of the Republic?'

'It was founded on reality.'

'My scanty acquaintance with your period does not allow me to dispute that statement with any fire, I fear. Whose dream, I wonder, laid those foundations?'

'Well, *dreams*, yes...'

'Poetic inspiration?'

'Well...'

Lord Jagged drew his great robe about him. 'Forgive me, Li Pao, for I realize that I *have* confused your argument. Please continue. I shall interrupt no further.'

But Li Pao had lost impetus. He fell into a sulking silence.

'There is a rumour, magnificent Lord Jagged, that you yourself have travelled in time. Do you speak from direct experience of Li Pao's period?' Mistress Christia raised her head from its contact with Gaf's groin.

'As a great believer in the inherent possibilities of the rumour as art,' said Lord Jagged gently, 'it is not for me to confim or deny any gossip you might have heard, sweet Mistress Christia.'

'Oh, absolutely!' She gave her full attention back to Gaf's anatomy.

Not without difficulty, Jherek held back from taxing Lord Jagged further on that particular subject, but Jagged continued:

'There are some who would argue that Time does not really exist at all, that it is merely our primitive minds which impose a certain order upon events. I have heard it said that everything is happening, as it were, concurrently. Some of the greatest inventors of time machines have used that theory to advantage.'

Jherek, desperately feigning lack of interest, poured himself a fresh tot. When he spoke, however, his tone was not entirely normal.

'Would it be possible, I wonder, to make a new time machine? If Shanalorm's or some other city's memories were reliable . . .'

'They are not!' The querulous voice of Brannart Morphail broke in. He had added an inch or two to his hump since Jherek had last encountered him. His club foot was decidedly over-done. He came limping across the floor, his smock covered in residual spots of the various substances in his laboratories. 'I have visited every one of the rotted cities. They give us their power, but their wisdom has faded. I was listening to your discourse, Lord Jagged. It is a familiar theory, favoured by the non-scientist. I assure you, none the less, that one gets nowhere with Time unless one treats it as linear.'

'Brannart,' said Jherek hesitantly, 'I was hoping to see you here.'

'Are you bent on pestering me further, Jherek? I have not forgotten that you lost me one of my best time machines.'

'No sign of it, then?'

'None. My instruments are too crude to detect it if, as I suspect, it has gone back to some pre-Dawn period.'

'What of the cyclic theory?' Lord Jagged said. 'Would you give any credence to that?'

'So far as it corresponds to certain physical laws, yes.'

'And how would that relate to the information we were

given by the Duke's little alien?'

'I had hoped to ask Yusharisp some questions – and so I might have done if Jherek had not interfered.'

'I am sorry,' said Jherek, 'but ...'

'You are living proof of the non-mutability of Time,' said Brannart Morphail. 'If you could go back and set to rights the events brought about by your silly meddling, then you would be able to prove your remorse. As it is, you can't, so I would ask you to stop expressing it!'

Pointedly, Brannart Morphail turned to Lord Jagged, a crooked, insincere grin upon his ancient features. 'Now, dear Lord Jagged, you were saying something about the cyclic nature of Time?'

'I think you are a little hard on Jherek,' said Lord Jagged. 'After all, My Lady Charlotina knew, to some extent, the outcome of her joke.'

'We'll speak no more of that. You wondered if Yusharisp's reference to the death of the cosmos – of the universe ending one cycle and beginning another – bore directly upon the cyclic theory?'

'It was a passing thought, nothing more,' said Lord Jagged, looking back over his shoulder and winking at Jherek. 'You should be kinder, Brannart, to the boy. He could bring you information of considerable usefulness in your experiments, surely? I believe you feel angry with him because his experiences are inclined to contradict your theories.'

'Nonsense! It is his interpretation of his experiences with which I disagree. They are naïve.'

'They are true,' said Jherek in a small voice. 'Mrs Underwood said that she would join me, you know. I am sure that she will.'

'Impossible – or, at very least, unlikely. Time does not permit paradoxes. The Morphail Theory specifically shows that once a time traveller has visited the future he cannot return to the past for any length of time; similarly any stay in the past is limited, for the reason that if he did stay there he could alter the course of the future and therefore produce chaos. The Morphail Effect is my term to describe an actual phenomenon – the fact that no one has ever been able to move backwards in Time and *remain* in the past. Merely because your stay in the Dawn Age was unusually long you cannot insist that there is a flaw in my description. The chances of your 19th-century lady being returned to this point in time are, similarly, very slight – millions to one. You could search for her, of course, through the millennia, and, if you were successful, bring her back here. She has no time machine of her own and therefore cannot control her flight into her future.'

'They had primitive time machines in those days,' Jherek said. 'There are many references to them in the literature.'

'Possibly, but *we* have never encountered another from her period. How she got here at all remains a mystery.'

'Some other time traveller brought her, perhaps?' Jherek was tentative, glad, at last, to have Brannart's ear. Privately, he thanked Lord Jagged for making it possible. 'She once mentioned a hooded figure who came into her room shortly before she found herself in our Age.'

'Yet,' said Morphail agitatedly, 'I have told you repeatedly that I have no record of a time machine materializing during the phase in which you claim she arrived. Since I last spoke with you, Jherek, I checked carefully. You are in error – or she lied to you ...'

'She cannot lie to me, as I cannot to her,' said Jherek simply. 'We are in love, you see.'

'Yes, yes! Play whatever games amuse you, Jherek Carnelian, but not at the expense of Brannart Morphail.'

'Ah, my wrinkled wonder-worker, can you not bring yourself to display a little more generosity towards our venturesome Jherek? Who else among us would dare the descent into Dawn Age emotions?'

'I would,' said Werther de Goethe, no longer in the distance. 'And with a better understanding of what I was doing, I would hope.'

'But your moods are dark moods, Werther,' said Lord Jagged kindly. 'They do not entertain as much as Jherek's!'

'I do not care what the majority thinks,' Werther told him. 'A more select group of people, I am told, think rather more of my explorations. Jherek has hardly touched on "sin" at all!'

'I could not understand it, vainglorious Werther, even when you explained it,' Jherek apologized. 'I have tried, particularly since it is an idea which my Mrs Underwood shared with you.'

'Tried,' said Werther contemptuously, 'and failed. I have not. Ask Mistress Christia.'

'She told me. I was very admiring. She will confirm —'

'Did you envy me?' A light of hope brightened Werther's doomy eye.

'Of course I did.'

Werther smiled. He sighed with satisfaction. Magnanimously he laid a hand upon Jherek's arm. 'Come to my tower some day. I will try to help you understand the nature of sin.'

'You are kind, Werther.'

'I seek only to enlighten, Jherek.'

'You will find it difficult, that particular task,' said Brannart Morphail spitefully. 'Improve his manners, Werther, and I, for one, will be eternally grateful to you.'

Jherek laughed. 'Brannart, are you not in danger of taking your "anger" too far?' He made a movement towards the scientist, who raised a six-fingered hand.

'No further petitions, please. Find your own time machine, if you want one. Persist in the delusion that your Dawn Age woman will return, if you wish. But do not, I beg you Jherek, involve me any further. Your ignorance is irritating and since you refuse the truth, then I'll have no more of you. I have my work.' He paused. 'If, of course, you were to bring me back the time machine you lost, then I might spare you a few moments.' And, chuckling, he began to return to his laboratories.

'He is wrong in one thing,' Jherek murmured to Lord Jagged, 'for they did have time machines in 1896, as you know. It was upon your instructions that I was placed in one and returned here.'

'Ah,' said Lord Jagged, studying the cloth of his sleeve. 'So you said before.'

'I am disconsolate,' said Jherek suddenly. 'You give me no direct answers (it is your right, of course) and Brannart refuses his help. What am I to do, Jagged?'

'Take pleasure in the experience, surely?'

'I seem to tire so easily of my pleasures, these days. And when it comes to ways of enjoying current experiences, my imagination flags, my brain betrays me.'

'Could your adventures in the past have tired you more than you realize?'

'I am certain it was you, Jagged, in 1896. It has occurred to me that even you are not aware of it!'

'Oh, Jherek, my jackanapes, what juicy abstractions you hint at! How close we are in temperament. You must expand upon your theories. Unconscious temporal adventurings!' Lord Jagged took Jherek's arm and led him back to where the main party had gathered.

'I base my idea,' began Jherek, 'on the understanding that you and I are good friends and that therefore you would not deliberately—'

'Later. I will listen later, my love, when our duties as guests are done.'

And again Jherek Carnelian was left wondering if Lord Jagged of Canaria were not, under his worldly airs, quite as confused as himself.

CHAPTER FOUR

TO THE WARM SNOW PEAKS

Bishop Castle had arrived late. He made a splendid entrance, in his huge head-dress twice as tall as himself and modelled on a stone tower of the Dawn Age. He had great, bushy red brows and long fine hair to match; it framed his saturnine features and fell to his chest. He wore robes of gold and silver and held the huge ornamental gearstick of some 21st-century religious order. He bowed to My Lady Charlotina.

'I left my contribution overhead, most handsome of hostesses. There were no others there, merely some flotsam on the surface. Am I to assume that I have missed the regatta?'

'You must, I am afraid.' My Lady Charlotina came towards him and took his long hand. 'But you shall have some of our naval fare.' She drew him towards the barrels of rum. 'Hot or cold?' she asked.

As Bishop Castle sipped the rum My Lady Charlotina described the battles which had taken place that day on Lake Billy the Kid. 'And the way in which Lady Voiceless's *Bismarck* sank my own *Queen Elizabeth* was ingenious, to say the least.'

'Scuppered below decks!' said Sweet Orb Mace with a relish for words which were meaningless to her. 'Hoisted by her holds. Spliced in her mainbrace! Belayed across the bows!' Her bright yellow, furry face became animated. 'Rammed,' she added, 'under the water-line.'

'Yes, dear. Your knowledge of nautical niceties is admirable.'

'Admiral!' giggled Sweet Orb Mace.

'Try a little less of the rum and a little more of the hard tack, dear,' suggested My Lady Charlotina, leading Bishop Castle to her hammock. Not without difficulty, he seated himself beside her (his hat was inclined to topple him over if he were not singularly careful). Bishop Castle noticed Jherek and waved his gearstick in a friendly greeting.

'Still pursuing your love, Jherek?'

'As best I can, mightiest of mitres.' Jherek left Lord Jagged's side. 'How are your giant owls?'

'Disseminated, I regret to say. I had it in mind to make a Vatican City in the same period as your London – I am a slave to fashion, as you know – but the only references I could find placed it on Mars about a thousand years later, so I must assume that it was not contemporary. A shame. A Hollywood I began came to nothing, so I gave up my efforts to emulate you. But when you are leaving, take a look at my ship. I hope you will approve of my careful research.'

'What is it called?'

'The *Mae West*,' said Bishop Castle. 'You know it, I

assume.'

'I do not! That makes it even more interesting.'

The Iron Orchid joined them, her features almost invisible in their glaring whiteness. 'We were considering a picnic in the Warm Snow Peaks, Charlotina. Would you care to come?'

'An exquisite idea! Of course I shall come. I think we have had the best of this entertainment now. And you, Jherek, will you go?'

'I think so. Unless Lord Jagged...' He turned to look for his friend, but Jagged had disappeared. He shrugged, reconciling himself. 'I would love it. It's ages since I visited the peaks. I had no notion that they still existed.'

'Weren't they something Mongrove made, in a lighter vein than usual?' Bishop Castle asked. 'Has anyone heard from Mongrove, by the by?'

'Not since he rushed off into space with Yusharisp,' the Iron Orchid told him, glancing about the hall. 'Where is the Duke of Queens? I had hoped he would wish to come with us.'

'One of his time travellers – he calls them "retainers", I understand – came to him with a message. The message animated him. He left with his eyes bright and his face flushed. Perhaps another traveller entering our Age?'

Jherek refused to be moved by this news. 'Did Lord Jagged go with him?'

'I am not sure. I wasn't aware he had gone.' My Lady Charlotina raised her slender eyebrows. 'Odd that he did not pay his respects. All this rushing and mystery whets my curiosity.'

'And mine,' said Jherek feelingly, but he was determined to remain as insouciant as possible and bide his time. If Amelia Underwood had come back, he would know soon enough. He rather admired his own self-control; he was even faintly astonished by it.

'Isn't the scenery piquant?' said the Iron Orchid with something of a proprietorial air. On the slope where they had laid their picnic they could see for scores of miles. Below, there were plains and rivers and lakes of a rich variety of gentle colours. 'So unspoiled. It hasn't been touched since Mongrove made it.'

'I must admit to a preference for his earlier work,' agreed Bishop Castle, running sensual fingers through the glittering snow which spread across the flanks of the great eminences. It was primarily white, with just the subtlest hint of pale blue. A few little flowers poked their delicate heads above the surface of the snow. They were mainly indigenous to this sort of alpine terrain – orange verdigris and yellow bottlewurt were two which Jherek had recognized, and another which he guessed was some kind of greenish St Buck's Buttons.

Sweet Orb Mace, who had insisted on accompanying them, was rolling down the slope in a flurry of warm snow, laughing and shouting and rather destroying the tranquillity of the scene. The snow clung to her fur as she tried to get up and instead she slipped and slid further, hanging, helpless with mirth, over a precipice which must have been at least a thousand feet high. Then, the snows gave way and with a startled yell she fell.

'What *could* have possessed Mongrove to go into space?' said My Lady Charlotina with a token smile in the general direction of the vanished Sweet Orb Mace. 'I cannot believe that she could possibly have been your father, you know, Jherek, however good the disguise.'

'It was a very strong rumour at one time,' the Iron Orchid said, stroking her son's hair and plucking little particles of snow from it. 'But I agree, Charlotina, it would not be quite in Sweet Orb Mace's style. Do you think she's all right?'

'Oh, of course. And if she forgot to use her gravity neutralizer, we can always resurrect her later. Personally, I am glad of the peace.'

'I understood from Mongrove that he regarded it as his destiny to accompany Yusharisp,' Bishop Castle said. 'To warn the universe of its peril.'

'I could never understand his pleasure in passing on such news,' said My Lady Charlotina. 'It could alarm some cultures, could it not? I mean, think of the timid creatures we have had to look after from time to time when they have visited us. Many of them are so frightened at seeing people who do not look like themselves that they rush off back to their own planets as soon as they can. If we do not, of course, select them for a menagerie. I suspect that Mongrove's motives were rather different. I suspect that he had become thoroughly bored with his gloomy rôle but was too proud to change.'

'An acute insight, sextupedal siren,' said Jherek. 'It is probably accurate.' He smiled, affectionately remembering the way in which he had tricked the giant when Mrs Amelia Underwood had belonged to Mongrove's menagerie. Then he frowned. 'Ah, those were pleasant days.'

'You are not happy with this outing, Jherek?' My Lady Charlotina was concerned.

'I can think of nowhere I would rather be in this whole world,' he said tactfully, producing a convincing smile.

Only the Iron Orchid was not entirely relieved to hear these words. She said quietly to him: 'I am inclined to regret the appearance both of Yusharisp from Space and your Mrs Underwood from Time. It could be imagination, but it seems to me at this moment that they introduced a certain flavour into our society which I find not entirely palatable. You were once the joy of us all, Jherek, because of the enthusiasm you carried with you...'

'I assure you, most considerate of mothers, that my enthusiasm burns within me still. It is merely that I have nothing on which to focus it at present.' He patted her hand. 'I promise to be more amusing just as soon as my inspiration returns.'

Relieved, she lay back in the snow, crying out almost immediately: 'Oh, look! It is the Duke of Queens!'

None could fail to recognize the air car which came lumbering over the peaks in their direction – a genuine ornithopter in the shape of a huge hen, clanking and clucking its way through the sky, sometimes dropping dangerously low and at other times soaring so high as to be almost invisible. Its wide wings beat mightily at the air, its mechanical head glared this way and that as if in horrible confusion. The beak opened and shut rapidly, producing a strange clashing noise. And there, just visible, was the Duke's head, adorned by a huge, wide-brimmed hat festooned with plumes, a hand waving a long silver spear, a scarlet cloak billowing about him. He saw them and, erratically, aimed his hen in their direction, coming in so close that they flung themselves into the snow so as to avoid being struck. The ornithopter spiralled upwards, then spiralled down again, landing, at last, a few yards away and waddling towards them.

The Duke's beard fairly bristled with excitement. 'It is a Hunt, my dears. Some of my beaters are not too far away. You must join me!'

'A Hunt, darling Duke – for what?' asked Bishop Castle, arranging his hat on his head.

'Another alien – same race as Yusharisp – spotted in these parts – spaceship and everything. We found the ship, but the alien had gone to ground somewhere. We'll find him soon. Bound to. Where's your car? Ah – Jherek's. That will do. Come along! The chase grows hot!'

They looked at one another enquiringly, laughingly. 'Shall we?' said My Lady Charlotina.

'It will be fun,' said the Iron Orchid. 'Will it not, Jherek?'

'Indeed, it will!' Jherek began to race towards his landau, the other three at his heels. 'Lead the way, hardiest of hunters. Into the air! Into the air!'

The Duke of Queens rattled his silver spear against his chicken's metal wattles. The chicken clucked and crowed and its wings began to beat again. 'Ha ha! What sport!'

The chicken rose a few feet and then came down again, after a false start. Snow blew about in clouds around the ornithopter and from out of this blizzard there came the sound of the Duke's exasperated tones mingling with the almost embarrassed voice of the chicken as it tried to lift its bulk skyward. Jherek's landau was already circling the air before the Duke had managed to take off.

'He always regretted letting me have Yusharisp,' said My Lady Charlotina. 'The alien did not seem much of an addition to a menagerie at the time. One can understand his pleasure at discovering another. I do hope he is successful. We must do our best to help him, everyone. We must take the Hunt seriously.'

'Without question!' said Jherek. More than the others, he welcomed the excitement.

'I wonder if this one bears the same dull tidings,' said the Iron Orchid. Only she did not seem to be as entertained by their escapade as much as she might have been.

CHAPTER FIVE

ON THE HUNT

From somewhere beyond a line of low, green hills there came the moan of a hunting harp.

The Duke's chicken was above and ahead of them, but they heard his thin voice crying:

'To the West! To the West!'

They saw him wave his spear in that direction, saw him desperately trying to turn his bird, which had begun to take on more than the suggestion of a list; so much that the Duke had great difficulty maintaining his seat.

A word from Jherek and the landau leapt forward, causing Bishop Castle to whistle with glee and hang hard onto his hat. The pleasure of the ladies was also keen;

they leant far over the sides, threatening to fall, as they sought the elusive alien.

'Be careful, my dears!' called Bishop Castle above the wail of the wind. 'Remember that these aliens can sometimes be dangerous. They have all sorts of *weapons*, you know!' He raised a cautioning hand. 'You could miss the fun, if killed or maimed, for there would not be time to resurrect you until the Hunt was finished.'

'We shall be careful, Bishop – oh, we *shall* be!' My Lady Charlotina chuckled as she almost lost her grip on the landau's rail.

'Besides, Jherek has a gun to protect us, haven't you, produce of my lust?' The Iron Orchid pointed at a rather large object on the floor of the landau. 'We were playing with it a day or two ago.'

'A deceptor-gun is not exactly a weapon,' said Bishop Castle, picking it up and squinting down its wide, bell-shaped funnel. 'All it can produce is illusions.'

'But they are very *real*, Bishop.'

The Bishop had taken an interest in the antique. 'One of the oldest examples I have seen. Notice that it even has its own independent power source – here, at the side.'

The others, having absolutely no interest in the Bishop's hobby, pretended that they had not heard him.

'Gone away!' came the Duke's distant drone. 'Gone away!'

'What *can* he mean?' said an astonished Lady Charlotina. 'Jherek, do you know?'

'I believe he means we have become too greatly separated,' Jherek offered. 'I have been deliberately keeping back, to give him the pleasure of the first sighting. It is his game, after all.'

'And quite a good one, really,' said My Lady Charlotina.

They passed the hills, drawing closer to the Duke of Queens.

'His ornithopter seems, as it were, on its last wings,' said Bishop Castle. 'Should we offer him a lift?'

'I don't think he would thank us,' said Jherek. 'We must wait until he crashes.'

They were flying over a landscape Jherek could not remember having seen before. It looked edible and was therefore probably something Argonheart Po had made. There were whole villages, after the Gentraxian fashion, set among wobbling clumps of golden trees.

'Mmm.' The Iron Orchid smacked her lips. 'I feel quite hungry again. Could we not taste . . .?'

'No time,' Jherek told her. 'I think I heard the harp again.'

The sky suddenly darkened and they sped through absolute blackness for a moment. Below them, they could detect the sound of a savage sea.

'We must be quite close to Werther's tower,' My Lady Charlotina suggested, re-arranging one of her several breasts, which had come loose.

And sure enough when the sky lightened to reveal boiling black clouds, there was Werther's mile-high monument to his moody ego.

'Those are the rocks,' said My Lady Charlotina, pointing at the base of the tower, 'where we found his body – dashed to fragments. Lord Jagged resurrected him. It took ages to gather all the pieces.'

Jherek remembered Sweet Orb Mace. If she had really fallen off the precipice, they should not leave her too long before restoring her.

The sun was shining again; the downs were green. 'There's the Earl of Carbolic's "Tokyo, 1901",' cried the Iron Orchid. 'What beautiful colours.'

'All reproductions of the original sea-shells,' Bishop Castle murmured knowingly.

The landau, dutifully following the Duke of Queens, veered suddenly and began to head towards the ground.

'He's down!' shouted Bishop Castle. 'Near that forest over there.'

'Is he hurt, Bishop?' The Iron Orchid was on the far side of the car.

'No. I can see him moving. He does not seem to be in a very good temper. He's hitting the ornithopter.'

'Poor thing.' My Lady Charlotina gasped as the landau bumped suddenly to earth.

Jherek left the carriage and began to walk towards the Duke of Queens. The Duke's hat was askew and one of his leggings was torn, but he was now, in all other respects, his normal self. He cast the spear aside, pushed back his hat, placed his hands on his hips and grinned at Jherek. 'Well, it was a good chase, eh?'

'Very stimulating. Your ornithopter is useless?'

'Utterly.'

The Duke of Queens felt it a point of pride to fly, for the most part, only authentic reproductions of ancient machines. He had often been counselled against the idea, but remained adamant – and much bruised.

'Can we take you back to your castle?' My Lady Charlotina asked.

'I'm not giving up. I'll continue the Hunt on foot. He'll be in those woods somewhere.' The Duke inclined his head in the direction of the nearby elms, cedars and mahoganies. 'My beaters will bring him towards us, if we're lucky. Will you come with me?'

Jherek shrugged. 'Willingly.'

They all began to march towards the woods and had gone a fair way before Bishop Castle lifted the deceptor-gun he still held in his hand. 'I'm sorry, I still have your antique. Shall I take it back, Jherek?'

'Bring it with you,' said Jherek. 'It might be useful in snaring the alien if we see him.'

'Good thinking,' said the Duke of Queens approvingly.

The wood was silent but for the faintest rustle of the leaves and the soft sounds of their footfalls on green, glowing moss. The trees smelled rich and sweet.

'Oh, isn't it *eerie*?' said My Lady Charlotina in breathless delight. 'A genuine old-fashioned Magic Wood. I wonder who made it.'

Jherek noticed that the quality of the light had

changed subtly, so that it was now a late summer evening; also the wood seemed to extend much further than he had at first supposed.

'It must be Lord Jagged's.' Bishop Castle removed his hat and stood leaning against it for a moment. 'Only he can capture this particular quality.'

'It does have Jagged's touch,' agreed the Iron Orchid, and she passed her arm through her son's.

'Then we must watch for mythical beasts,' said the Duke of Queens. 'Kangaroos and the like, if I know Jagged.'

The Iron Orchid squeezed Jherek's arm. 'I think it's getting darker,' she whispered.

CHAPTER SIX

THE BRIGAND MUSICIANS

The foliage above their heads was now so thick that hardly any light came through at all. The silence had deepened and, scarcely realizing what they were doing, they all crept as quietly as possible over the moss, gently pushing aside the low branches which increasingly blocked their way.

My Lady Charlotina took Jherek's other arm, murmuring animatedly: 'We are like the babes in the bush. Do you think we will be *lost*, Jherek?'

'It would be wonderful if we were,' said the Iron Orchid, but Jherek said nothing. For some reason, the mysterious wood had a healing effect upon his emotions.

He felt much calmer; more at ease than he had been for a long while. He wondered why the thought had occurred to him that he was, in this wood, somehow much closer to Mrs Underwood. He peered through the shadowy gloom, half-expecting to see her in her grey dress and straw hat, standing beside the bole of a cedar or a pine, smiling at him, ready to continue where she had left off with what she termed his 'moral education'.

Only the Duke of Queens was unaffected by the atmosphere. He paused, tugging at his black beard, and he frowned.

'The beaters must have detected something,' he complained. 'Why haven't we heard them?'

'The forest does seem to be rather larger than we had at first supposed.' Bishop Castle tapped his fingers against the barrel of the deceptor-gun. 'Could we be walking in the wrong direction, I wonder?'

Jherek and the two ladies had also stopped. Jherek himself was in something of a trance. It had been in a wood not dissimilar to this one where Mrs Amelia Underwood had kissed him, admitting, at last, her love for him – and from a wood like this one she had been whisked away, back to her own time. For a moment he considered the notion that Lord Jagged and My Lady Charlotina had planned a surprise for him, but it was obvious from My Lady Charlotina's behaviour that she had known nothing about this wood before they had discovered it. Jherek took a deep breath of the air. The predominant smell, he supposed, was of earth.

'What was that?' The Duke of Queens cupped a hand to his ear. 'A harp, was it?'

Bishop Castle had abandoned his hat altogether now. He scratched his red locks, turning this way and that. 'I think you're right, my dear Duke. Music, certainly. But it could be birds.'

'The song of the rabbit,' gasped My Lady Charlotina, romantically clasping her various hands over her multitude of breasts. 'To hear it in these woods is to become

Primordial Man – experiencing the exact emotions He experienced all those millions of years ago!'

'You are in a lyrical mood indeed, my lady,' lazily suggested Bishop Castle, but it was obvious that he, too, was infected by the atmosphere. He raised the hand in which he held the heavy deceptor-gun. 'I think the sound came from that direction.'

'We must go extremely quietly,' said the Iron Orchid, 'to be sure not to disturb either the alien or any wild-life.' Jherek suspected that she did not care a jot about disturbing the animals – she merely desired the same uninterrupted peace which he had been enjoying. He confirmed her words by means of a grave nod.

A little later they detected a haze of dancing crimson light ahead of them and they proceeded with even greater caution.

And then the music began.

It dawned on Jherek, after a few moments, that this was the most beautiful music he had ever heard. It was profound, stately and very moving, it hinted at harmonies beyond the harmonies of the physical universe, it spoke of ideals and emotions which were magnificent in their sanity, their intensity and their humanity; it took him through despair and he no longer despaired, through pain and he no longer felt pain, through cynicism and he knew the exhilaration of hope; it showed him what was ugly and it was no longer ugly; he was dragged into the deepest chasms of misery only to be lifted higher and higher until his body, mind and feelings were in perfect balance and he knew an immeasurable ecstasy.

As he listened, Jherek, with the others, moved into the haze of crimson light; their faces were bathed in it, their clothing coloured by it, and they saw that it and the music emanated from a glade. The glade was occupied by a large machine and it was this which was the source of the crimson glow; it stood lopsidedly upon four or five spindly legs, one of which at least was evidently broken. The body was asymmetrical but essentially pear-shaped with little glassy protuberances, like flaws in a piece of ceramic, dotted about all over it; from an octagonal object at the tip, the crimson poured. Near the crippled machine stood or sat seven humanoid beings who were unmistakably space-travellers – they were small, scarcely half Jherek's size, and burly, with heads akin in shape to that of their ship, with one long eye containing three pupils which darted about, sometimes converging, sometimes equidistant, with large, elephantine ears, with bulbous noses. They were bewhiskered, unkempt and dressed in a variety of garments, none of which seemed congruent with another. And it was from these little men that the music came, for they held instruments of unlikely shapes, which they plucked or blew or sawed at with stumpy fingers. At their belts were knives and swords and on their wide, splayed feet were heavy boots; their heads were decorated with caps, scarves or metal helmets, adding to their practical appearance. Jherek found it difficult to equate the exquisite beauty of the music with the ruffians who produced it.

All were affected by the music, listening in awe, unnoticed by the players, as the symphony slowly reached a resolution of apparently clashing themes, ending in a concordance which was at once unimaginably complex and of an absolute simplicity. For a moment there was silence. Jherek realized that his eyes were full of tears and, glancing at the others, he saw that they had all been as moved as he had been. He drew a series of deep breaths, as a man near-drowned when he breaks at last to the surface of the sea, but he could not speak.

The musicians for their part threw aside their instruments and lay back upon the ground roaring with laughter. They giggled, they shrieked, they slapped their sides, they were nearly helpless with mirth – and their laughter was raucous, it was even crude, as if the musicians had been enjoying a sing-song of lewd lyrics rather than playing the most beautiful music in the universe. Gabbling in a harsh, grating language, they whistled parts of the melodies, nudging one another, winking and bursting into fresh fits of merriment, holding their sides and groaning as they shook.

Somewhat put out by this unexpected sequel, the Duke of Queens led his party into the glade. At his appearance the nearest alien looked up, pointed at him, snorted and fell into another series of convulsions.

The Duke, who had always made a fetish of inconvenience, flicked on his wrist translator (which had originally been intended for communicating with Yusharisp's colleague), an ornate, old-fashioned and rather bulky piece of equipment he favoured over simpler forms of translator. When the aliens' outburst had subsided and they sat asprawl, still tittering and giggling a little, the Duke bowed, presenting himself and his companions to them.

'Welcome to our planet, gentlemen. May we congratulate you on a performance which went beyond pleasure?'

As he drew closer, Jherek detected an odour he recognized from his sojourn in the 19th century; it was the smell of stale sweat. When one of the aliens stood up at last and came swaggering towards them, the odour grew decidedly stronger.

Grinning, the ruffian scratched himself and offered them a bow which was a mockery of the Duke's and sent his companions into a complaining, painful sequence of snorts and grunts.

'We were just having a bit of fun among ourselves,' the alien said, 'to pass the time. There seems precious little else to do on this tired old globe of yours.'

'Oh, I'm sure we can find ways of amusing you,' said My Lady Charlotina. She licked her lips. 'How long have you been here?'

The alien stood on one bandy leg and scratched at his calf. 'Not long. Sooner or later we'll have to see about repairing our ship, I suppose.' He offered her what seemed to be a crude wink. My Lady Charlotina sucked in her lower lip and sighed, while the Iron Orchid whispered to Jherek:

'What marvellous additions they will make to a menagerie. I believe the Duke realizes it, too. He has first claim, of course. A shame.'

'And from what part of the cosmos have you come?' asked Bishop Castle politely.

'Oh, I doubt if you'd recognize the name. I'm not even sure it exists any more. Me and my crew are the last of our species. We're called the Lat. I'm Captain Mubbers.'

'And why do you travel the spaces between the stars?' The Iron Orchid exchanged a secret look with My Lady Charlotina. Their eyes sparkled.

'Well, you probably know that this universe is pretty much crapped out now. So we're drifting, really, hoping to find the secret of immortality and get a bit of fun along the way. When that's done – if we ever succeed – we're going to try to escape into another universe not subject to the same conditions.'

'A second universe?' said Jherek. 'Surely a contradiction?'

'If you like.' Captain Mubbers shrugged and yawned.

'The secret of immortality and a bit of fun!' exclaimed the Duke of Queens. 'We have both! You must be our guests!'

It was now quite plain to Jherek that the devious Duke intended to add the whole band to his collection. It would be a real feather in his cap to own such splendid musicians, and would more than make up for his gaff involving Yusharisp. However, Captain Mubbers' response was not quite what the Duke seemed to hope for. An expression of low cunning crossed his features and he turned to his crew.

'What do you think, lads? This gentleman says we can stay at his place.'

'Well,' said one, 'if he's *really* got the secret of immortality...'

'He's not just going to give it up, is he?' said another. 'What's in it for him?'

'We assure you, our motives are altruistic,' Bishop Castle insisted. 'It would give us pleasure to have you as our guests. Say that we enjoy your music. If you play some more for us, we will show our gratitude by making you immortal. *We* are all immortal, aren't we?' He turned for confirmation to his companions who chorused their agreement.

'Really?' mused Captain Mubbers. He fingered his jaw.

'Really,' breathed the Iron Orchid. 'Why I myself am some . . .' She cleared her throat, suddenly aware of My Lady Charlotina's affected lack of interest in her remarks. 'Well, quite a few hundred years old,' she concluded anticlimatically.

'I have lived two or three thousand years, at least,' said the Duke of Queens.

'Don't you get bored?' enquired one of the seated aliens. 'That's what we were wondering about.'

'Oh, no. No, no, no! We have our pastimes. We create things. We talk. We make love. We invent games to play. Sometimes we'll go to sleep for a few years, maybe longer, if we do tire of what we're doing, but you'd be surprised how swiftly the time goes when you're immortal.'

'I'd never even thought of it,' said Bishop Castle. 'I suppose it's because people have been immortal on this planet for millennia. You get used to it.'

'I've a better idea,' Captain Mubbers said with a grin. 'You will be *our* guests. We'll take you with us as we continue our ride through the universe. On the way you can tell us the secret of immortality.'

Nonplussed, the Duke shuddered. 'To space! Our nerves would not bear it, I regret!' He turned with a wan smile to Jherek, still addressing the alien. 'I thank you for your invitation, Captain Mubbers, but we have to refuse. Only Mongrove, who seeks discomfort in all forms, would ever contemplate venturing into *space*.'

'No,' said My Lady Charlotina sweetly. 'It is *our* duty to entertain you. We shall all go back to Below-the-Lake and have, oh, a party.'

'We were having a party when you turned up,' Captain Mubbers pointed out. He sniffed and rubbed at his bulbous nose. 'Mind you, I think I know what you mean. Eh?' And he sidled up to her and gave her a nudge in the thigh. 'We've been a long time in space, lady.'

'Oh, you poor things!' said My Lady Charlotina, putting two of her hands on either side of his face and twiddling his moustachios. 'Are there no females of your race now?'

'Not so much as a single old slag.' He raised his eyes piteously to contemplate the trees. 'It's been a very hard trip, you know. Why, I doubt if I've tickled an elbow in four or five years.' He darted a chiding glance at his companions who were leering to a man. Then, smirking, he reached up and put his hand on her bottom. 'Why don't you and me go inside the ship and talk about this some more?'

'It would be more comfortable if you returned with us,' insisted the Duke of Queens. 'You could have some food, a rest, a bath...'

'Bath?' Captain Mubbers started in alarm. 'Do what? Come off it, Duke. We've still got a long way to go. What are you trying to suggest?'

'I mean that we can supply anything you desire. We could even create females of your own species for you, reproduce exactly your own environment. It is easily within our power.'

'Ho!' said Captain Mubbers suspiciously. 'I bet!'

'I'd like to know what their game is.' One of the crew got up, picking his teeth (which were pointed and yellow). His three pupils darted this way and that, regarding the five Earth-people. 'You're too sodding eager to please, if you ask me.'

The Duke made a vague gesture with his hands. 'Surely you can't suspect our motives? As guests on our planet, it is your right to be entertained by us.'

'Well, you're the first lot who thought that,' said the crew member, putting his hand into his shirt and rubbing his chest. 'No, I agree with the skipper. You come with us.' The others nodded their approval of this proposal.

'But,' the Iron Orchid told them reasonably, 'my scrumptious little space-sailors, you fail to understand our absolute *loathing* of these vacuous reaches. Why, hardly anyone makes the trip to the nearer planets of our own system any more, let alone plunging willy-nilly into that chilly wilderness *between* the stars!' Her expression softened, she removed the cap of the one who had just approached. She stroked his bald spot. 'It is no longer in our natures to leave the planet. We are set in our ways. We are an old, old race, you see. Space bores us. Other planets irritate and frustrate us because good manners demand that we do not re-model them to our own tastes. What is there for us in your infinity? After all, save for minor differences, one star looks very much like another.'

The Lat snatched his hat from her hand and pulled it down over his head. 'Thrills,' he said. 'Adventures. Peril. New sensations.'

'There *are* no new sensations, surely?' said Bishop Castle, willing to hear of one if it existed. 'Just modifications of the old ones, I'd have thought.'

'Well,' said Captain Mubbers decisively, stooping to pick up his instrument. 'You're coming with us and that's that. I know a trap when I smell one.'

The Duke of Queens pursed his lips. 'I think it's time we left. Evidently, an impasse...'

'More like a *fait accompli*, chummy,' said the pugnacious alien, pointing his instrument in the Duke's general direction. 'Get 'em down and shove 'em up!'

By this time the other Lat had picked their horns and strings from the ground.

'I don't follow you?' the Duke told Captain Mubbers. 'Get what down? And shove what up?'

'The trousers and the hands in that order,' said Captain Mubbers. And he motioned with his instrument.

Bishop Castle laughed. 'I believe they are *menacing* us,

you know!'

My Lady Charlotina gave a squeal of delight. The Iron Orchid put fingers to her lips, her eyes widening.

'Are those weapons as well as musical instruments?' asked Jherek with interest.

'Spot on,' said Captain Mubbers. 'Watch this.' He turned away, directing the oddly shaped device at the nearby trees. 'Fire,' he said.

A howling, burning wind issued from the thing in his hands. It seared through the trees and turned them to smoking ash. It produced a tunnel of brightness through the gloom of the forest; it revealed a plain beyond, and a mountain beyond that. The wind did not stop until it reached the far-away mountain. The mountain exploded. They heard a faint bang.

'All right?' said Captain Mubbers, turning back to them enquiringly.

His companions smirked. One of them, in a metal helmet, said: 'You wouldn't get far, would you, if you tried to run for it?'

'Who would resurrect us?' said Bishop Castle. 'How curious? I haven't seen an actual weapon before.'

'You intend, then, to *kidnap* us!' said My Lady Charlotina.

'Mibix unview per?' said Captain Mubbers. 'Kroofrudi! Dyew oh tyae, hiu hawtquards!'

In despair, the Duke of Queens had switched off his translator.

CHAPTER SEVEN

A CONFLICT OF ILLUSIONS

'It is certainly not very much of an advantage,' said the Duke of Queens miserably. They all sat together near the spaceship while the Lat kneeled nearby, absorbed in some kind of gambling game. The Iron Orchid and My Lady Charlotina seemed to be the stakes. Only My Lady Charlotina was getting impatient.

She sighed. 'I do wish they'd hurry up. They're lovable, but they're not very decisive.'

'You think not?' said Bishop Castle, picking at some moss. 'They seemed to have reached the decision to kidnap us pretty quickly.'

Jherek was miserable. 'If they take us into space I'll

never see Mrs Amelia Underwood!'

'Try a disseminator ring on their weapons again,' suggested the Iron Orchid. 'Mine doesn't work, Bishop, but yours might.'

The Bishop concentrated, fiddling with his ring, but nothing at all happened. 'They are only effective on things we create ourselves. We could get rid of the rest of the trees, I suppose ...'

'There seems little point,' said Jherek. He sighed.

'Well,' said the Duke of Queens, an inveterate viewer of the bright side, 'we might see something interesting in space.'

'Our ancestors never did,' the Iron Orchid reminded him. 'Besides, how are we to get back?'

'Build a spaceship.' The Duke of Queens was puzzled by her apparent obtuseness. 'With a power ring.'

'If they work in the depths of the cosmic void. Do you recall any record of the rings themselves being used away from Earth?' Bishop Castle shrugged, not expecting a reply.

'Did they have power rings all those thousands and thousands of years ago? Oh, dear, I feel very sleepy.' My Lady Charlotina was unusually bored. She had gone off the whole idea of making love to the Lat, either singly or all together. 'Let's create an air car and go, shall we.'

Bishop Castle was grinning. 'I have a more amusing notion.' He waved the deceptor-gun. 'It should cheer us all up and make an exciting end to this adventure. Presumably the gun is conventionally loaded, Jherek?'

'Oh, yes.' Jherek nodded absently.

'Then it will fire illusions at random. I remember the craze for these toys. Two players each have a gun, not knowing which illusions will come out, but hoping that one illusion will counter another.'

'That's right,' said Jherek. 'I couldn't find anyone interested enough to play, however.'

Captain Mubbers had left his men and was swaggering towards them.

Hujo, ri fert glex min glex viel,' he barked, menacing them at musical instrument point.

They pretended to have no idea at all as to his meaning (which was fairly clear – he wanted the ladies to enter the spaceship).

'Kroofrudi!' said Captain Mubbers. 'Glem min glex viel!'

My Lady Charlotina dimpled prettily. 'My dear captain, we simply can't understand you. And you can't understand us now, can you?'

'Hrunt.' Shifting his grip on his instrument, Captain Mubbers smiled salaciously and placed a bold hand on her elbow. 'Hrunt glex, mibix?'

'Dog!' My Lady Charlotina blushed and fluttered her eyelashes at him. 'I suppose we should try the gun now, Bishop.'

There came a slight 'pop' and everything turned to blue and white. Blue and white birds and insects, delicate, languid, flitted through equally delicate willow trees – white against blue or blue against white, depending on their particular background.

Captain Mubbers was a little surprised. Then he shook his head and pushed My Lady Charlotina towards the ship.

'Perhaps we should allow him just a brief ravishment,' she said.

'Too late,' said Bishop Castle, and he fired again. 'Who loaded this gun, Jherek? We must hope for something a little less restrained.'

The second illusion now intruded upon the first. Into the delicate blue and white scenery there lumbered a monstrous ten-legged beast which was predominantly reptilian, with huge eyes which shot flames as it turned its fierce head this way and that.

Captain Mubbers yelled and aimed his instrument. He managed to destroy a fair amount of the wood beyond the blue and white landscape and the flame-eyed monster, but they were unaffected.

'I think it's time to slip away,' said Bishop Castle, pulling the trigger once more and introducing bright abstract patterns which whizzed erratically through the air, clashing horribly with the blue and white and making the reptilian beast irritable. The Lat were firing repeatedly at the monster, backing away from it as it advanced (by luck) towards them.

'Oh,' said the Iron Orchid in disappointment as Jherek took her by the arm and dragged her into the forest, 'can't we watch?'

'Can you remember where we left your air car, Jherek?' The Duke of Queens was panting and excited. 'Isn't this fun?'

'I think it was that way,' Jherek replied. 'But perhaps it would be wise to stop and make another?'

'Would that be sporting, do you think?' asked the Iron Orchid.

'I suppose not.'

'Come on then!' She raced off through the trees and had soon vanished in the gloom. Jherek followed her, with Bishop Castle close on his heels.

'Mother, I'm not sure it's wise to separate.'

Her voice drifted back to him. 'Oh, Jherek, you've become joyless, my juice!'

But soon he had lost her altogether and he stopped, exhausted, beside a particularly large old tree. Bishop Castle had kept up with him and now handed him the deceptor-gun. 'Would you mind holding this for a bit, Jherek. It's quite heavy.'

Jherek took it and tucked it into his clothes. He heard the sound of something large blundering through the forest. Trunks fell, branches cracked, fires started.

'It's particularly realistic, isn't it?' Bishop Castle seemed almost of the impression that he had made the monster himself. He winced as something howled past his nose and destroyed a line of trees. 'The Lat seem to be catching up with us.' He dived into the undergrowth, leaving Jherek still undecided as to the direction he should take.

And now, because he might be killed forever, before he could see Mrs Amelia Underwood again, he was filled by panic. It was a new emotion and part of his mind took an objective curiosity in it. He began to run. He was careless of the branches which struck his face. He ran on and on, through darkness, away from the sounds and the destruction. Danger was a wall which seemed to surround him, in escaping one source he encountered another. Once he bumped against someone in the dark and was about to speak when they said, 'Ferkit!' He moved away as quietly as possible and heard a blood-chilling shriek from somewhere else.

He ran, he fell, he crawled, got up and ran again. His chest was painful and his brain was useless. He thought that he might be sobbing and he knew that the next time he would fall and not have the will to rise.

He tripped. He lost his balance. He was reconciled to Death. He went sprawling down the sides of an old pit, bits of earth and rock falling with him, and was about to congratulate himself that he might after all have found relative safety when the bottom of the pit gave way and he was sliding down something which was smooth and plainly built for this purpose. Down and down he slid on the metal chute, feeling sick with the speed of his descent, unable to reach his power rings, unable to slow himself, until he must have been almost a mile underground. Then, at last, the chute came to an end and he landed, winded and dazed, on what appeared to be a pile of mildewed quilts.

The light was dim and it was artificial. After a while he sat up, feeling tenderly over his body for broken bones, but there were none. A peculiar sense of well-being filled him and he lay back upon the quilts with a yawn, hoping that his friends had managed to get back to the landau. He would rest and then consider the best method of joining them. A power ring would doubtless bore a tunnel upwards for him, then he could drift to the surface by means of counter-gravity. He felt extremely sleepy. He could hardly believe in the events which had just taken place. He was about to close his eyes when he heard a small, lisping voice saying:

'Welcome, sir, to Wonderland!'

He looked round. A small girl stood there. She had large blue eyes and blonde curly hair. Her expression was demure.

'You're very well made,' said Jherek admiringly. 'What are you, exactly?'

The small girl's expression was now one of disgust. 'I'm a little girl, of course. Aren't I?'

CHAPTER EIGHT

THE CHILDREN OF THE PIT

Jherek stood up and dusted at his white draperies, saying kindly: 'Little girls have been extinct for thousands of years. You're probably a robot or a toy. What are you doing down here?'

'Playing,' said the robot or toy; then it stepped forward and kicked his ankle, 'And I know what I am. And I know what you are. Nurse said we had to be careful of grown-ups – they're dangerous.'

'So are little girls,' said Jherek feelingly, rubbing an already battered leg. 'Where is your Nurse, my child?'

He had to admit he was surprised at how lifelike the creature was, but it could not be a child or he would have heard about it. Save for himself and Werther de Goethe, children had not been born on Earth for millennia. People were created, as the Duke of Queens had created Sweet Orb Mace, or re-created themselves, as King Rook had become Bishop Castle. Having children, after all, was rather a responsibility. Creating mature adults was difficult enough!

'Come on,' said the being, taking his hand. She led him down a tunnel of pink marble which, to Jherek's eye, had something in common with the style and materials of the ancient cities, though the tunnel seemed relatively new. The tunnel opened into a large room crammed with beautiful reproductions of antiques, some of which Jherek recognized as miniature whizz-mobiles, rocking horses, furry partridges, seasores, coloured quasimodos and erector sets. 'This is one of our play-rooms,' she told him. 'The school-room is through there. Nurse should be out soon with the others. *I'm* playing truant,' she added proudly.

Jherek admired his surroundings. Someone had gone to considerable trouble to reproduce an old nursery. He wondered if this, like the wood above, could be attributed to Lord Jagged. It certainly showed his finesse.

Suddenly a door opened and into the room poured a score of boys and girls, all of about the same apparent age, the boys in shirts and shorts, the girls in frilly dresses and aprons. They were shouting and laughing, but they stopped when they saw Jherek Carnelian. Their eyes widened, their mouths hung open.

'It's an adult,' said the self-styled child. 'I caught it in one of the corridors. It fell through the roof.'

'Do you think it's a Producer?' asked one of the boys, stepping up to Jherek and looking him over.

'They're fatter than that,' another girl said. 'Here comes Nurse, anyway. She'll know.'

Behind them loomed a tall figure, grim of visage, clothed in grey steel, humanoid and stern. A robot, much larger than Jherek, built to resemble a middle-aged woman in the costume of the Late Multitude Cultures. Her voice, when she spoke, was a trifle rusty and her limbs were inclined to creak when they moved. Cold blue eyes glared from the steel face.

'What's this, Mary Wilde, playing truant again?' Nurse tut-tutted 'And who's this other little boy. Not one of mine by the look of him.'

'We think it's an adult, Nurse,' said Mary Wilde.

'Nonsense, Mary. Your imagination is running away with you again. There are no such things as adults any more.'

'That's what *he* said about children.' Mary Wilde put her hand to her mouth to suppress a giggle.

'Pull yourself together, Mary,' said Nurse. 'I can only conclude that this young man has also been playing truant. You will both be punished by having only bread and milk for supper.'

'I assure you that I *am* an adult, madam,' Jherek insisted. 'Although I have been a child in my time. My name is Jherek Carnelian.'

'Well, you're reasonably polite at any rate,' said Nurse. Her lips clashed as she drew them together. 'You had better meet the other little boys and girls. I really can't think why they've sent me an extra child. I'm already two over my quota.' The robot seemed a shade on the senile side, unable to accept new information. Jherek had the impression that she had been performing her tasks for a considerable length of time and had, as robots will in such conditions, become set in her ways. He decided, for the moment, to humour her.

'This is Freddie Fearless,' said Nurse, laying a gentle metal hand upon the brown curly locks of the nearest boy. 'And this is Danny Daring. Mick Manly and Victor Venture, here. Gary Gritt, Peter Pluck and Ben Bold, there. Kit Courage – Dick Dreadnought – Gavin Gallant. Say hello to your new friend, boys.'

'Hello,' they chorused obediently.

'What did you say your name was, lad?' asked Nurse.

'Jherek Carnelian, Nurse.'

'A strange, unlikely name.'

'Your children's names all seem to have a certain similarity, if I may say so...'

'Nonsense. Anyway, we'll call you Jerry – Jerry Jester, Always Playing the Fool, eh?'

Jherek shrugged.

'And these are the girls – Mary Wilde, you've already met. Betty Bold, Ben's sister. Molly Madcap. Nora Nosie.'

'I'm the school sneak,' announced Nora Nosie with undisguised pleasure.

'Yes, dear, and you're very good at it. This is Gloria Grande. Flora Friendly. Katie Kinde – Harriet Haughtie – Jenny Jolly.'

'I am honoured to meet you all,' said Jherek, with something of Lord Jagged's grace. 'But perhaps you could tell me what you are doing underground?'

'We're hiding!' whispered Molly Madcap. 'Our parents sent us here to escape the movie.'

'The movie?'

'Pecking Pa the Eighth's *The Great Massacre of the First-Born* – that's the working title, anyway,' Ben Bold told him.

'It's a remake about the birth of Christ,' said Flora Friendly. 'Pecking Pa is going to play Herod himself.'

This name alone meant something to Jherek. He knew that he had met a time traveller once who had fled from this same Pecking Pa, the Last of the Tyrant Producers, when he had been in the process of making another drama about the eruption of Krakatoa.

'But that was thousands of years ago,' Jherek said. 'You couldn't have been here all that time. Or could you?'

'We work to a weekly shift here,' said Nurse. She turned her eyes towards a chronometer on the wall. 'If we don't hurry, I shall be late with the recycling. That's the trouble with the parents – they've no thought for me – they send down another child without ever thinking about my schedules – and then they wonder why the routines are upset.'

'Do you mean you're recycling *time*?' asked Jherek in amazement. 'The same week over and over again.'

'Until the danger's over,' said Nurse. 'Didn't your parents tell you? We'll have to get you out of those silly clothes. Really, some mothers have peculiar ideas of how to dress children. You're quite a big boy, aren't you. It will mean making a shirt and shorts for a start.'

'I don't want to wear a shirt and shorts, Nurse! I'm not sure they'll suit me.'

'Oh, my goodness! You *have* been spoiled, Jerry!'

'I think the danger *is* over, Nurse,' said Jherek desperately, backing away. 'The Age of the Tyrant Producers has long since past. We're now very close to the End of Time itself.'

'Well, dear, that won't affect us here, will it? We operate a neat closed system. It doesn't matter what happens in the rest of the universe, we just go round and round through the same period. I do it all myself, you know, with no help from anyone else.'

'I think you've become a little fixed in your habits, Nurse. Have you considered limbering up your circuits?'

'Now, Jerry, I'll assume you're not being deliberately rude, because you're new here, but I'm afraid that if I hear any more talk like that from you I'll have to take strong measures. I'm kind, Jerry, but I'm firm.'

The great robot rumbled forward on her tracks, reaching out her huge metal arms towards him. 'Next, we'll undress you.'

Jherek bowed. 'I think I'll go now, Nurse. But as soon as I can I'll return. After all, these children can begin to grow up, the danger being over. They'll want to see the outside world.'

'Language, boy!' bellowed Nurse fiercely. 'Language!'

'I didn't mean to ...' Jherek turned and bolted.

'Soldiers of the Guard!' roared Nurse.

Jherek found his way blocked by huge mechanical toy soldiers. They had expressionless faces and were not anything like as sophisticated as Nurse, but their metal bodies effectively blocked his escape.

Jherek yelped as he felt Nurse's strong hands fall on him. He was yanked into the air and flung over a cold steel knee. A metal hand rose and fell six times on his bottom and then he was upright again and Nurse was patting his head.

'I don't like to punish boys, Jerry,' said Nurse. 'But it is for their own good that they do not leave the nursery. When you are older you will understand that.'

'But I *am* older,' said Jherek.

'That's impossible.' Nurse began to strip his clothes from him and moments later he stood before her wearing the same kind of shirt and shorts and knee-socks as Kit Courage, Freddie Fearless and the others. 'There,' she said in satisfaction, 'now you're not so much of an odd boy out. I know how children hate to be different.'

Jherek, twice the height of his new chums, knew then that he was in the power of a moron.

CHAPTER NINE

NURSE'S SENSE OF DUTY

Jherek Carnelian sat at the far end of the dormitory, a bowl of bread and milk in his lap, an expression of hopeless misery upon his face, while Nurse stood by the door saying goodnight.

'I really should point out, Nurse, that, since your closed environment has been entered by an outsider, a variety of temporal paradoxes are likely to take place. They are sure to disrupt your way of life and mine probably much more than we should want.'

'Sleepy time now,' said Nurse firmly, for the sixth time since Jherek had arrived. 'Lights out, my little men!'

Jherek knew that it was useless to get up once he had

gone to bed. Nurse would detect him immediately and put him back again. At least it was easy to know how long he had been here. Each day measured exactly twenty-four hours and each hour had sixty minutes – it was all on the old non-malleable reckonings. The Age of the Tyrant Producers would have been one of the last to use them. Jherek knew that Nurse must have been programmed to act upon new information and to deal with it intelligently, but she had become sluggish over the centuries. His only hope was to keep insisting on what was self-evident truth, but it could take months. He wondered how the Iron Orchid and the others had fared on the surface. With any luck, when he was able to escape, he would find the Lat weapons neutralized (it was quite easy to do and had been done on several previous occasions) and the aliens returned to space.

'I think you should consider a re-programming, Nurse!' Jherek called into the darkness.

'Now, now, Jerry, you know I disapprove of cheeky children.' The door closed. Nurse rolled away down the corridor.

Jherek wondered if he had been right in believing that he had detected a faint uncertainty in Nurse's voice to-night.

Freddie Fearless said admiringly from the next bed. 'You can certainly keep it up, can't you Jerry? I don't know why the old girl lets you get away with it.'

'Perhaps, in her subconscious, she realizes that I'm an adult and doesn't like to admit it,' Jherek suggested.

This drew a ripple of laughter from the boys.

'That's Jerry Jester,' said Dick Dreadnought, 'always playing the fool! Life wouldn't be nearly so much fun without you, Jerry.' Like the others, he had accepted Jherek immediately and seemed to have forgotten that he had only recently entered the nursery.

With a sigh, Jherek turned over and tried to operate his power rings, as he had taken to doing every night, but plainly some protective device in the nursery blocked off the source of their energy. He still had the deceptor-gun, but he couldn't think of any use for it at present. He felt under his pillow. It was still there. With a sigh, he tried to go to sleep. It seemed to him that he was in an even more uncomfortable situation than when he had been Snoozer Vines' prisoner in Jone's Kitchen in 1896. He remembered that there, too, they had called him Jerry. Did all gaolers favour that name for him?

Jherek wakened and was surprised that the lights were not on, as they usually were; also he could not smell breakfast; moreover Nurse was not standing by the door ringing her bell and calling 'Wake up, sleeepyheads!' as was her wont.

From somewhere beyond the dormitory, however, there came various noises – yells, explosions, screams and bangs – and suddenly the door had sprung open, admitting light from the corridor.

'Berchoos ek!' said a familiar voice. 'Hoody?'

And Captain Mubbers, his whiskers bristling, his musical instrument in his hands, stood framed in the doorway. He glared at Jherek.

'Kroofrudi!' he said in recognition, and a nasty grin appeared on his face.

Jherek groaned. The Lat had found him and now the children were in danger.

'Ferkit! Jillip goff var heggo heg, mibix?'

'I still can't understand you, Captain Mubbers,' Jherek told the brigand-musician. 'However, I take it you would like me to accompany you and, of course, I shall. Hopefully you will then leave the rest of – I mean – leave the children alone.' With as much dignity as he could muster considering he was wearing a jacket and trousers of brightly striped flannel far too small for him, he rose from his bed, his hands in the air, and walked towards the Lat captain.

Captain Mubbers snorted with mirth. 'Shag uk fang dok pist kickle hrunt!' he yelled. His men gathered around him and they, too, joined in their leader's merriment. One even dropped his weapon, but was quick to recover it again. This made Jherek wonder if their own power source came from their spaceship or if the weapons, like his deceptor-gun, had independent cells. He supposed that there wasn't an easy way of finding out. He bore their laughter as manfully as he could.

Captain Mubbers' bulbous nose fairly glowed with the strain of his laughter. 'Uuuungh, k-k-kroofrudi! Uuuuuungh, k-kroofrudi!'

'What's this? What's this? More naughty boys from outside!' came Nurse's booming voice from down the corridor. 'And during the night, now! This will *never* do!'

Captain Mubbers and his men looked at one another with expressions of disbelieving surprise on their faces. Nurse rolled steadily on.

'You are nasty rough boys and you are disturbing my charges. Haven't you homes to go to?'

'Kroofrudi!' said Captain Mubbers.

'Ferkit!' said another.

'Ugh! Disgusting!' said Nurse. 'Where do you pick up such words!'

Captain Mubbers stepped to the head of his gang and menaced Nurse with his instrument. She ignored it completely. 'I have never seen such filthy little boys. And what have you got in your hands? Catapults, no doubt!'

Captain Mubbers aimed his instrument at Nurse and pulled the trigger. Howling fire left the muzzle and struck Nurse full on her chest. She made a fussy, brushing motion, then one of her arms extended and she snatched the instrument from Captain Mubbers' grasp.

'Naughty, naughty, naughty, little boy. I will not have such behaviour in the nursery!'

'Olgo glex mibix?' said Captain Mubbers placatingly. He tried to smile, but his eyes were glassy as he stared up at Nurse whose huge metal head looked down upon him. 'Frads kolek goj sako!'

'I will listen to no more of your nastiness. This is the only way to teach manners to the likes of you, young man.'

With great satisfaction, Jherek watched as Captain Mubbers was snatched yelling into the air, was thrown across Nurse's knee, was divested of his trousers and slapped soundly upon his bare and unlovely backside. Captain Mubbers shouted to his crew to help and they all began kicking at Nurse, tugging at her, swearing at her, to no avail. Sedately she completed the punishment of Captain Mubbers and then, one by one, gave similar treatment to his companions, confiscating their instruments at the same time.

Chastened, they all stood holding their bottoms, red-faced and tearful, while Jherek and the boys from the dormitory laughed delightedly.

Nurse began to roll down the corridor with an armful of alien instruments. 'You may have these back only when you leave the nursery,' she said. 'And you will not leave the nursery until you have learned some manners!'

'Kroofrudi,' said Captain Mubbers, glowering at the disappearing robot, but he spoke the word softly, nervously, more from bravado than anything else. 'Hrunt!'

Jherek felt almost sorry for the Lat, but he was glad that the children were safe.

'I heard you!' Nurse called chidingly. 'I shan't forget!'

Captain Mubbers caught her drift. He said no more.

Jherek grinned. It pleased him more than he would have guessed to see the Lat brought so low. 'Well,' he said, 'we're all in the same kettle of fish now, eh?'

'Mibix?' queried Captain Mubbers in a small, defeated voice.

'However, the idea of spending the same week, recycled through eternity, in the company of children, Lat and a senile robot is not entirely appealing,' said Jherek, in a critical and miserable mood for him. 'I really must think how I'm to effect my escape and achieve a reconciliation with Mrs Amelia Underwood.'

Captain Mubbers nodded. 'Greef cholokok,' he said, by way of affirmation.

Nurse was returning. 'I've locked your toys away,' she told Captain Mubbers and the others. 'And now it's straight to bed without any supper. Have you any idea how late it is?'

The Lat stared at her blankly.

'My goodness, I do believe they've sent me a party of mentally subnormals!' exclaimed Nurse. 'I thought they were going to be left behind to placate Pecking Pa.' She pointed at the row of empty beds down one side of the dormitory. 'In there,' she said slowly. 'Bed.'

The Lat shuffled towards the beds and stood looking stupidly down at them.

Nurse sighed and picked up the nearest alien, stripping off his clothing and plumping him down, pulling the bedding over his shivering body. The others hastily began to pull off their own clothes and climbed into bed.

'That's more like it,' said Nurse. 'You're learning.' She turned her hard, blue eyes on Jherek. 'Jerry, I think you'd better come to my sitting room. I'd like a word with you now.'

Meekly, Jherek followed Nurse down the corridor and into a room whose walls were covered in flock wallpaper, with landscape paintings and little ornaments. Elsewhere was a great deal of chintz and gingham. It reminded Jherek vaguely of the house he had furnished for Mrs Amelia Underwood.

Nurse rolled to one corner of the room. 'Would you like a cup of tea, Jerry?'

'No thank you, Nurse.'

'You are probably wondering why I asked you here, when it's long past your bed-time.'

'It had occurred to me, Nurse, yes.'

'Well,' she announced, 'my creative-thinking circuits are beginning to come back into play, I think. I've become rather set in my ways, as old robots will, particularly when involved in a temporal recycling operation like this one. You follow me?'

'I do indeed.'

'You are older than the other children, so I think I can talk to you. Even,' Nurse made an embarrassed rumbling sound somewhere inside her steel chest, 'even ask your advice. You think I've become a bit of a stick in the mud, don't you?'

'Oh, not really,' Jherek told her kindly. 'We all develop habits, over the millennia, which are sometimes hard to lose when we no longer need them.'

'I have been thinking about one or two things which you've said this past week. You've been to the surface, evidently.'

'Um...'

'Come now, lad, tell the truth. I shan't punish you.'

'Yes, I have, Nurse.'

'And Pecking Pa is dead?'

'And forgotten.' Jherek wriggled uncomfortably in his too-tight pyjamas. 'It's been thousands of years since the Age of the Tyrant Producers. Things are much more peaceful these days.'

'And these outsiders – they are from the outside time-phase?'

'They are, more or less.'

'Which means that paradoxes begin to occur, if we're not careful.'

'I gather so, from what I have been told about the nature of Time.'

'You've been informed correctly. It means that I must think very carefully now. I knew this moment would come eventually. I have to worry about my children. They are all I have. They are the Future.'

'Well, the Past, at least,' said Jherek.

Nurse glared sternly at him. 'I'm sorry, Nurse,' he said. 'That was facetious of me.'

'My duty is to take them into an age where they will be in no danger,' Nurse continued. 'And it seems that we have reached that age.'

'I am sure they will be very welcome in my society,' Jherek told her. 'I and one other are the only ones who have been children. My people love children. I am proof of that.'

'They are gentle?'

'Oh, yes, I think so. I'm not quite sure of the meaning – you use words which are archaic to me – but I think "gentle" is a fair description.'

'No violence?'

'There you've lost me altogether. What is "violence"?'

'I'm satisfied for the moment,' said Nurse. 'I must be grateful to you, Jerry Jester. For all that you are always acting the fool, you're made of decent stuff underneath. You've re-awakened me to my chief responsibilities.' Nurse seemed to simper (as much as a robot could simper). 'You are my Prince Charming, really. And I was the Sleeping Beauty. It would seem that the danger to the children is over and they can be allowed to grow normally. What sort of conditions exist in the outside world. Will they find good homes?'

'Any kind they wish,' said Jherek.

'And the climate. Is it good?'

'Whatever one cares to make it.'

'Educational facilities?'

'Well,' he said, 'I suppose you could say that we believe in self-education. But the facilities are excellent. The libraries of the rotted cities are still more or less intact.'

'Those other children. They seemed to know you. Are they from your time?' It was plain that Nurse was becoming increasingly intelligent with every passing second.

'They are aliens from another part of the galaxy,' Jherek said. 'They were chasing me and some of my friends.' He explained what had happened.

'Well, they must be expelled, of course,' said Nurse, having listened gravely to his account. 'Preferably into another period of time where they can do no more harm. And here normal time must replace recycled time. That is merely a question of stopping a process . . .' Nurse sank into a thoughtful silence.

Jherek had begun to hope. 'Nurse,' he said. 'Forgive me for interrupting, but am I to understand that you have the power to pass people back and forth in Time?'

'Back is very difficult – they are not inclined to stick, in my experience. Forth is much easier. Recycling is,' a mechanical chuckle sounded in her throat, 'child's play, as it were.'

'So you could send me back, say, to the 19th century?'

'I could. But the chances of your staying there for long are poor...'

'I'm aware of the theory. We call it the Morphail Effect in this age. But you could send me back.'

'I could, almost certainly. I was programmed specifically for Time Manipulation. I probably know more about it than any other being.'

'You would not have to use a time machine?'

'There's a chamber in this complex, but it would not be a machine which moved physically through time. We've abandoned such devices. As a matter of fact, time travel itself, being so uncertain, was pretty much abandoned, too. It was only in order to protect the children that we built this place.'

'Would you send me back, Nurse?'

Nurse seemed hesitant. 'It's very dangerous, you know. I know that I owe you a favour. I feel stupid for having forgotten my duty. But sending you so far back...'

'I have been before, Nurse. I'm aware of the dangers.'

'That's as may be, young Jerry Jester. You were always a wild one – though I could never be as firm with you as I should have been. How I used to laugh, privately, here in my little sitting room, at your antics, at the things you said...'

'Nurse! I think you're slipping again,' Jherek warned her.

'Eh? Put another lump of coal on the fire, would you my boy?'

Jherek looked around, but could see no fire.

'Nurse?'

'Aha!' said Nurse. 'Send you to the 19th century. A long time ago. A long, long time ago. Before I was born. Before *you* were born, that's for certain. In those days there were oceans of light and cities in the skies and wild flying beasts of bronze. There were herds of crimson cattle that roared and were taller than castles. There were shrill...'

'To 1896 to be precise, Nurse. Would you do it for me? It would mean a great deal.'

'Magics,' she continued, 'phantasms, unstable nature, impossible events, insane paradoxes, dreams come true, dreams gone awry; nightmares assuming reality. It was a rich time and a dark time...'

'1896, Nurse.'

'Ah, sometimes, in my more Romantic moments, I wish that I had been some merchant governess; some great lady of Hong Kong, trading capital of the world, where poets, scholars and soldiers of fortune all congregated. The ships of a hundred nations at anchor in the harbours. Ships from the West, with cargoes of bearskins and exotic soaps; ships from the South, with crews of dark-visaged androids, bearing bicycles and sacks of grit; ships from the East...'

'Plainly we share an interest in the same century,' said Jherek desperately. 'Do not deny me my opportunity to go back there, dear Nurse.'

'How could I?' Her voice had become almost inaudible, virtually soft as nostalgia seized her. At that moment, Jherek felt a deep sympathy for the old machine; it was rare that one was privileged to witness the dreams of a robot. 'How could I refuse my Jerry Jester anything. He has made me live again.'

'Oh, Nurse!' Jherek was moved to tears. He ran forward and hugged the rigid body. 'And with your help I, too, shall come to life again!'

CHAPTER TEN

ON THE BROMLEY ROAD AGAIN

'Producing the time jump is relatively easy,' said Nurse, studying a bank of instruments in her laboratory as Jherek came rushing in (he had returned, briefly, to his ranch to get some translator pills and study his records in order to make himself a suit of clothes which would not set him apart from the denizens of 1896). 'Oh, that's yours, by the way. I found it under your pillow when I was making your bed.' The old robot pointed at the deceptor-gun resting on one of her benches. With a murmur of thanks, Jherek picked it up and slipped it into the pocket of his black overcoat. 'The problem is,' Nurse went on, 'in getting the spacial co-ordinates correctly fixed. A city called London (I'd never heard of it until you mentioned it) in an island called England. I've had to consult some pretty ancient memory banks, I can tell you, but I think it's sorted out now.'

'I can go?'

'You were always an impatient one, Jerry.' Nurse laughed affectionately. She still seemed to have it implanted in her that she had brought Jherek up since he had been a young boy. 'But – yes – I think you can set off soon. I do hope you're aware of the dangers, however.'

'I am, Nurse.'

'What on earth are you wearing, my boy? It looks like something I once saw in Tyrant Pecking Pa's remake of the classic *David Copperfield Meets the Wolf Man*. I considered it rather fanciful, then. But Pecking Pa always ran to *emotional* authenticity rather than period exactitude, I was told. At least, that's what he used to say. I met him once, you know. Some years ago, when his father was still alive. His father was so different; a gentleman. You wouldn't have known they were related. His father made all those wonderful, charming movies. They were a joy to live through. The whole society took part, of course. You'd be far too young to remember the pleasure of having even a small part in *Young Adolf Hitler* or *The Four Loves of Captain Marvel*. When Pecking Pa VIII came to power all the romance vanished. Realism became the rage. And someone suffers, every time, during a Realism period (I mean, who supplies the blood? Not the Tyrant himself!)'

Privately, Jherek Carnelian was very grateful to Pecking Pa VIII for his excesses in the name of Realism. Without them, Nurse would not be here now.

'The stories were pretty much the same, of course,' said Nurse, fiddling with some controls and making a screen turn to liquid gold, 'only more blood. There, that should do it. I hope there was just the one location for London on this island of yours. It's very *small*, Jerry.' She turned her great metal head to look at him. 'What I would call a bit of a low-budget country.'

Jherek wasn't, as usual, following her too clearly. But he nodded and smiled.

'Still, small productions quite often produced interesting pictures,' said Nurse, with a touch of condescension. 'Hop into the box, Jerry, there's a good lad. I'll be sorry to see you go, but I suppose I'll have to get used to it, now. I wonder how many will remember their old Nurse in a few years time. Still, it's a fact of life I have to face. Starlets must become stars some day.'

Jherek stepped gingerly into the cylindrical chamber in the middle of the laboratory.

'Goodbye, Jerry,' said Nurse's voice from outside, before the buzzing became too loud, 'try to remember everything I taught you. Be polite. Listen for your cues. Keep away from casting couches. Camera! Action!'

And the cylinder seemed to begin to spin (though it might have been Jherek spinning). He clapped his hands to his ears to keep out the noise. He groaned. He fainted.

He moved through a country that was all soft, shifting colours and whose people were bodiless, kindly with sweet voices. He fell back and he was falling through the fabric of the ages, down and down to the very beginnings of mankind's long history.

He felt pain, as he had felt it before, but he did not mind it. He knew depressions such as he had never experienced, but they did not concern him. Even the joy which came to him was a joy he did not care about. He knew that he was borne upon the winds of Time and he knew, beyond any question, that at the end of this journey he would be reunited with his lost love, the beautiful Mrs Amelia Underwood. And when he reached 1896 he would not allow himself to be sidetracked from his great Quest for Bromley, as he has been sidetracked before by Snoozer Vines.

He heard his own voice calling, ecstatic and melodic. 'Mrs Underwood! Mrs Underwood! I am coming! Coming! Coming!'

And at last the sensation of falling had stopped and he opened his eyes, expecting to find himself still in the cylinder, but he was not. He was lying upon soft grass under a large, warm sun. There were trees and not far off the glint of water. He saw people walking about, all dressed in costumes appropriate to the late 19th century – men and women, children, dogs. In the distance he saw a carriage go by, drawn by horses. One of the inhabitants started to stroll slowly, purposefully towards him and he recognized the man's suit. He had seen many such during his previous stay in 1896. Quickly he slipped his hand in his pocket, took out a translator pill and popped it into his mouth. He began to stand up.

'Excuse me, sir,' said the man heavily, 'but I was wondering as to whether you could *read*.'

'As a matter of fact,' began Jherek, but was cut off.

'Because I was looking at that there notice, not four yards off, which plainly states, if I'm not mistaken, that you are requested not to set foot on this particular stretch of lawn, sir. Therefore, if you would kindly return to the public walk, I for one would be relieved to inform you that you had returned to the path of righteousness and were no longer breaking one of the byelaws of the Royal Borough of Kensington. Moreover, I must point out, sir, that if I was ever to catch you committing the same felony in this here park, I would be forced to take your name and address and see that a notice to appear in court on a particular date was served on you.' And the man laughed. 'Sorry, sir,' he said in a more natural tone, 'but you shouldn't really be on the grass.'

'Aha!' said Jherek. 'I follow. Thank you, um – officer – that's it, isn't it? It was inadvertent ...'

'I'm sure it was, sir. You being a Frenchman, by your accent, wouldn't understand our ways. It's more free and easy over there, of course.'

Jherek stepped rapidly to the path and began to walk in the direction of a pair of large marble gate-posts he could see in the distance. The policeman fell in beside him, chatting casually about France and other foreign places he had read about. Eventually, he saluted and walked off down another path, leaving Jherek wishing that he had enquired the way to Bromley.

At least, thought Jherek, it was a relief not to be attracting quite so much attention as he had during his last trip to the Dawn Age. People still glanced at him from time to time and he felt rather self-conscious, as one might, but he was able to walk along the street and enjoy the sights without interruption. Carriages, hansoms, dairymen's drays, tradesmen's vans, all went by, filling the air with the creak of axles, the clopping of horses' hooves, the rattling of the wheels. The sun was bright and warm and the smells of the street had a very different quality to the one they had had during Jherek's previous stay. He realized that it must be summer now. He paused to smell some roses which were spilling over the wall of the park. They were beautiful. There was a *texture* to the scent which he had never been able to reproduce. He inspected the leaves of a cypress and here, too, found that his own work lacked a certain subtlety of detail which was difficult to define. He found himself delighting, even more than before, in the beauties of 1896. He stopped to stare as a two-storeyed omnibus went by, pulled by huge, muscular horses. On the open top deck be-ribboned straw hats nodded, sunshades twirled and blazers blazed; while below, through dusty windows and a confusion of advertisements, sat the dourer travellers, their eyes upon their newspapers and penny magazines. Once or twice a motor car would wheeze past, its exhaust mingling with the dust from the street, its driver swathed in a long coat and white cap, in spite of the heat, and Jherek would watch it in smiling wonderment.

He removed his top hat, wondering why his face seemed damp, and then he realized to his delight that he was *sweating*. He had witnessed this phenomenon before, in the inhabitants of this period, but had never dreamed of experiencing it personally. Glancing at the faces of the people who passed by – all in different stages of youth or decay, all male or female (without choice, he remembered, with a thrill of excitement) – he saw that many of them were sweating, too. It added to his sense of identification with them. He smiled at them, as if to say 'Look, I am like you,' but, of course, they did not understand. Some, indeed, frowned at him, while two ladies walking together giggled and blushed.

He continued along the road in a roughly eastward direction, noticing that the traffic grew thicker. The park ended on his left and a fresh one appeared on his right. Boys with bundles of newspapers and placards began to run about shouting, men with long poles began to poke them into lanterns which stood on thin, tall pedestals at regular intervals along the sides of the pavement, and the air became a little cooler, the sky a little darker.

Jherek, realizing that night was falling and that he had become so entranced by the atmosphere that he was, again, in danger of being deflected from his path, decided that it was time to make for Bromley. He remembered that Snoozer Vines had told him that he would need to take a train and that the trains left from somewhere called 'Victoria' or possibly 'Waterloo'.

He went up to a passer-by, a portly gentleman dressed rather like himself who was in the process of purchasing a newspaper from a small boy.

'Excuse me, sir,' said Jherek, raising his hat, 'I wonder if you would be good enough to help me.'

'Certainly, sir, if I can,' said the portly gentleman genially, replacing his money in his waistcoat pocket.

'I am trying to reach the town of Bromley, which is in Kent, and I wondered if you knew which train station I would need.'

'Well,' said the portly gentleman with a frown. 'It will either be Victoria or Waterloo, I should think. Or possibly London Bridge. Possibly all three. I would suggest that you purchase a railway guide, sir. I can see from the cut of your jib that you're a stranger to our shores – and an investment, if you intend to travel about this fair island, in a railway guide will pay you handsome dividends in the long run. I am sorry I cannot be of more assistance. Good evening to you.' And the portly gentleman rolled away, calling out:

'Cab! Cab!'

Jherek sighed and continued to walk up the busy street which seemed to become increasingly densely populated with every passing moment. He wished that he had mastered the logic of reading when he had had the chance. Mrs Underwood had tried to teach him, but she had never really explained the principles to his satisfaction. With the logic fully understood, a translation pill would do the rest for him, working its peculiar re-structuring effect upon his brain-cells.

He tried to stop several people, but they all seemed too busy to want to talk to him, and at last he reached an intersection crammed with traffic of every description. Bewildered he came to another stop, staring over the hansoms, four-wheelers and carts at the statue of a naked bowman with wings on his ankles, doubtless some heroic aviator who had taken part in the salvation of London during one of its periodic wars with other of the island's city-states. The noise was almost overwhelming, and now darkness added to his confusion. He thought he recognized some of the buildings and landmarks, from his last trip to the past, but he could not be sure. They were inclined to look very much alike. Across the street he saw the gold and crimson front of a house which seemed, for some reason, more as he had originally imagined 19th century houses to be. It had large windows with lace curtains from behind which poured warm gaslight. Other curtains, of red velvet held by cords of woven gold, were drawn back from the windows and from within there came a number of pleasant smells. Jherek decided that he would give up trying to stop one of the busy passers-by and ask for help, instead, at one of these houses. Nervously, he plunged into the traffic, was missed first by an omnibus, then by a hansom cab, then by a four-wheeler, was cursed at roundly by almost everyone and arrived panting and dusty on the other side of the road.

Standing outside the gold and crimson building, Jherek realized that he was not sure of how to begin making his enquiry. He saw a number of people go through the doors as he watched, and concluded that some sort of party was taking place. He went to one of the windows and peered, as best he could, through the lace curtains. Men in black suits very much like his own, but wearing large white aprons around their waists, hurried about, bearing trays of food, while at tables, some large and some small, sat groups of men and women, eating, drinking and talking. It was definitely a party. Here, surely, would be someone who could help him.

As he stared, Jherek saw that at a table in the far corner sat a group of men, dressed in slightly different style to most of the others. They were laughing, pouring foaming wine from large green bottles, having an animated conversation. With a shock, Jherek thought that one of the men, dressed in a light yellow velvet jacket, a loose scarlet cravat covering a good deal of his shirt front, bore a startling resemblance to his old friend Lord Jagged of Canaria. He seemed to be on familiar terms with the other men. At first Jherek told himself that this could only be Lord Jagger, the judge at his trial, and decided that he could see points about the handsome, lazy face which distinguished him from Jagged, but he knew that he deceived himself. Obviously coincidence could explain the resemblance, both of name and features, but here was his opportunity to decide the truth. He left the windows and pushed open the doors of the house.

Immediately a small, dark man approached him.

'Good evening, sir? You have a table?'

'Not with me,' said Jherek in some astonishment.

The small man's smile was thin and Jherek knew enough to understand that it was not particularly friendly. Hastily, he said: 'My friends – over there!'

'Ah!' This seemed sufficient explanation. The small man was relieved. 'Your hat and coat, sir?'

Jherek realized that he was supposed to give these items of clothing to the man as some form of surety. Willingly, he dispensed with them, and made his way as quickly as possible to the table where he had seen Jagged.

But, somehow, Jagged had managed to disappear again.

A man with a coarse, good-natured face, adorned by a large black moustache, looked up at Jherek enquiringly. 'How d'ye do?' he said heartily. 'You'd be M. Fromental, from Paris? I'm Harris – and this is Mr Wells, whom you wrote to me about.' He indicated a narrow-faced, slight man, with a scrubby moustache and startlingly bright pale blue eyes. 'Wells, this is the agent chap Pinker mentioned. He wants to handle all your work over there.'

'I'm afraid...' began Jherek.

'Sit down my dear fellow and have some wine.' Mr Harris stood up, shaking his hand warmly, pressing him downwards into a chair. 'How are all my good friends in Paris? Zola? I was sorry to hear about poor Goncourt. And how is Daudet, at present? Madame Rattazzi is well, I hope.' He winked. 'And be sure, when you return, to give my regards to my old friend the Comtesse de Loynes...'

'The man,' said Jherek, 'who was sitting across the table from you. Do you know him, Mr Harris?'

'He's a contributor to the *Review* from time to time, like everyone else here. Name of Jackson. Does little pieces on the arts for us.'

'Jackson?'

'Do you know his stuff? If you want to meet him, I'll be glad to introduce you. But I thought your interest in coming to the Café Royale tonight was in talking to H. G. Wells here. He's a rather larger gun, these days, eh, Wells?' Mr Harris roared with laughter and slapped Mr Wells on the shoulder. The quieter man smiled wanly, but he was plainly pleased by Harris's description.

'It's a pity so few of our other regular contributors are here tonight,' Harris went on. 'Kipling said he'd come, but as usual hasn't turned up. A bit of a dour old dog, y'know. And nothing of Richards for weeks. We thought we were to be blessed by a visitation from Mr Pett Ridge, too, tonight. All we can offer are Gregory, here, one of our editors.' A gangling young man who grinned as, unsteadily, he poured himself another glass of champagne. 'And this is our drama critic, name of Shaw.' A red-bearded, sardonic looking man with eyes almost as arresting as Mr Wells's, dressed in a suit of tweeds which seemed far too heavy for the weather, acknowledged the introduction with a grave bow from where he was seated at the far end of the table looking over a bundle of printed papers and occasionally making marks on them with his pen.

'I am glad to meet all of you, gentlemen,' said Jherek Carnelian desperately. 'But it is the man – Mr Jackson, you called him – who I am anxious to speak to.'

'Hear that, Wells?' cried Mr Harris. 'He's not interested in your fanciful flights at all. He wants Jackson. Jackson!' Mr Harris looked rather blearily about him. 'Where's Jackson gone? He'll be delighted to know he's read in Paris, I'm sure. We'll have to put his rates up to a guinea an item if he gets any more famous.'

Mr Wells was frowning, staring hard at Jherek. When he spoke, his voice was surprisingly high. 'You don't look too well, M. Fromental. Have you recently come over?'

'Very recently,' said Jherek. 'And my name isn't Fromental. It's Carnelian.'

'Where on earth is Jackson?' Mr Harris was demanding.

'We're all a bit drunk,' said Mr Wells to Jherek. 'The last of the copy's gone off and Frank always likes to come here to celebrate.' He called to Mr Harris. 'Probably gone back to the office, wouldn't you say?'

'That's it,' said Mr Harris satisfied.

'Would you kindly refrain from making so much

damned noise, Harris!' said the red-headed man at the far end of the table. 'I promised these proofs back by tonight. And where's our dinner, by the way?'

Mr Wells leaned forward and touched Mr Harris on the arm. 'Are you absolutely sure this chap Fromental's turning up, Harris? I should have left by now. I've some business to attend to.'

'Turning up? He's here, isn't he?'

'This appears to be a Mr Carnelian,' said Mr Wells dryly.

'Oh, really? Well, Fromental will turn up. He's reliable.'

'I didn't think you knew him personally.'

'That's right,' Mr Harris said airily, 'but I've heard a lot about him. He's just the man to help you, Wells.'

Mr Wells seemed sceptical. 'Well, I'd better get off, I think.'

'You won't stay to have your supper?' Mr Harris was disappointed. 'There were one or two ideas I wanted to discuss with you.'

'I'll drop round to the office during the week, if that's all right,' said Mr Wells, rising. He took his watch from his waistcoat pocket. 'If I get a cab I ought to make it to Charing Cross in time for the nine o'clock train.'

'You're going back to Woking?'

'To Bromley,' said Mr Wells. 'Some business I promised to clear up for my parents.'

'To Bromley, did you say?' Jherek sprang from his chair. 'To Bromley, Mr Wells?'

Mr Wells was amused. 'Why, yes. D'you know it?'

'You are going now?'

'Yes.'

'I have been trying to get to Bromley for – well, for a very long time. Might I accompany you?'

'Certainly.' Mr Wells laughed. 'I never heard of anyone who was eager to visit Bromley before. Most of us are only too pleased to get away from it. Come on, then, Mr Carnelian. We'll have to hurry!'

CHAPTER ELEVEN

A CONVERSATION ON TIME MACHINES AND OTHER TOPICS

Although Mr Wells's spirits seemed to have lifted considerably after he had left the Café Royale, he did not speak much until they had left the cab and were safely seated in a second class carriage which smelled strongly of smoke. At the ticket office Jherek had been embarrassed when he was expected to pay for his fare, but Wells, generously supposing him to have no English money, had paid for them both. Now he sat panting in one corner while Jherek sat opposite him in the other. Jherek took a wondering curiosity in the furnishings of the carriage. They were not at all as he had imagined them. He noted little stains and tears in the upholstery and assured himself that he would reproduce them faithfully at the next opportunity.

'I am extremely grateful to you, Mr Wells. I had begun to wonder if I should ever find Bromley.'

'You have friends there, have you?'

'One friend, yes. A lady. Perhaps you know her?'

'I know one or two people still, in Bromley.'

'Mrs Amelia Underwood?'

Mr Wells frowned, shook his head and began to pack tobacco into his pipe. 'No, I'm afraid not. What part does she live in?'

'Her address is 23 Collins Avenue.'

'Ah, yes. One of the newer streets. Bromley's expanded a lot since I was a lad.'

'You know the street?'

'I think so, yes. I'll put you on your way, don't worry.' Mr Wells sat back with his eyes twinkling. 'Typical of old Harris to confuse you with someone else he'd never met. For some reason he hates to admit that he doesn't know someone. As a result he claims to know people he's absolutely no acquaintance with, they hear that he's spoken of them as if they were his dearest friends, get offended and won't have anything to do with him!' Mr Wells's voice was high-pitched, bubbling, animated. 'I'm inclined to be a bit in awe of him, none the less. He's ruined half-a-dozen papers, but still publishes some of the best stuff in London – and he gave me a chance I needed. You write for the French papers do you, Mr Carnelian?'

'Well, no...' said Jherek, anxious not to have a repetition of his previous experience, when he had told the absolute truth and had been thoroughly disbelieved. 'I travel a little.'

'In England?'

'Oh, yes.'

'And where have you visited so far?'

'Just the 19th century,' said Jherek.

Mr Wells plainly thought he had misheard Jherek, then his smile broadened. 'You've read my book!' he said ebulliently. 'You travel in time, do you, sir?'

'I do,' said Jherek, relieved to be taken seriously for once.

'And you have a time machine?' Mr Wells's eyes twinkled again.

'Not now,' Jherek told him. 'In fact, I'm looking for one, for I won't be able to use the method by which I arrived, to return. I'm from the future, you see, not the past.'

'I see,' said Mr Wells gravely. The train had begun to move off. Jherek looked at identical smoke-grimed roof after identical smoke-grimed roof illumined by the gas-lamps.

'The houses all seem to be very similar and closely packed,' he said. 'They're rather different to those I saw earlier.'

'Near the Café Royale? Yes, well you won't have slums in your age, of course.'

'Slums?' said Jherek. 'I don't think so.' He was enjoying the jogging motion of the train. 'This is great fun.'

'Not quite like your monorails, eh?' said Mr Wells.

'No,' said Jherek politely. 'Do you know Mr Jackson, Mr Wells? The man who left when I arrived.'

'I've seen him once or twice. Had the odd chat with him. He seems interesting. But I visit the *Saturday Review*'s offices very infrequently – usually when Harris insists on it. He needs to *see* his contributors from time to time, to establish their reality, I think.' Mr Wells smiled in anticipation of his next remark. 'Or perhaps to establish his own.'

'You don't know where he lives in London?'

'You'll have to ask Harris that, I'm afraid.'

'I'm not sure I'll have the chance now. As soon as I find Mrs Underwood we'll have to start looking for a time machine. Would you know where to find one, Mr Wells?'

Mr Wells's reply was mysterious. 'In here,' he said, tapping his forehead with his pipestem. 'That's where I found mine.'

'You built your own?'

'You could say that.'

'They are not common in this period, then?'

'Not at all common. Indeed, some critics have accused me of being altogether too imaginative in my claims. They consider my inventions not sufficiently rooted in reality.'

'So time machines are just starting to catch on?'

'Well, mine seems to be catching on quite well. I'm beginning to get quite satisfactory results, although very few people expected it to go at first.'

'You wouldn't be prepared to build me one, would you, Mr Wells?'

'I'm afraid I'm more of a theorist than a practical scientist,' Mr Wells told him. 'But if you build one and have any success, be sure to let me know.'

'The only one I travelled in broke. There was evidence, by the way, to suggest that it came from a period two thousand years before this one. So perhaps you are actually *re*-discovering time travel.'

'What a splendid notion, Mr Carnelian. It's rare for me to meet someone with your particular quality of imagination. You should write the idea into a story for your Parisian readers. You'd be a rival to M. Verne in no time!'

Jherek hadn't quite followed him. 'I can't write,' he said. 'Or read.'

'No true Eloi should be able to read or write.' Mr Wells puffed on his pipe, peering out of the window. The train now ran past wider-spaced houses in broader streets as if some force at the centre of the city had the power to condense the buildings, as clay is condensed by centrifugal force as it is whirled on the potter's wheel. Jherek was hard put to think of any explanation and finally dismissed the problem. How, after all, could he expect to understand Dawn Age aesthetics as it were overnight?

'It's a shame you aren't doing my translations, M. Carnelian, you'd do a better job, I suspect, than some.

You could even improve on the existing books!'

Again unable to follow the animated words of the young man, Jherek Carnelian gave up, merely nodding.

'Still, it wouldn't do to let oneself get too far-fetched, I suppose,' Mr Wells said thoughtfully. 'People often ask me where I get my incredible ideas. They think I'm deliberately sensational. They don't seem to realize that the ideas seem very *ordinary* to me.'

'Oh, they seem exceptionally ordinary to me, also!' said Jherek, eager to agree.

'Do you think so?' piped H. G. Wells a little coldly.

'Here we are, Mr Carnelian. This is your fabulous Bromley. We seem to be the only visitors at this time of night.' Mr Wells opened the carriage door and stepped out onto the platform. The station was lit by oil-lamps which flickered in a faint breeze. At the far end of the train a man in uniform put a whistle to his lips and blew a shrill blast, waving a green flag. Mr Wells closed the door behind them and the train began to move out of the station. They walked past boxes full of flowers, past a white-painted fence, until they came to the exit. Here an old man accepted the tickets Mr Wells handed him. They crossed the station precinct and entered a street full of two-storey houses. A few gas-lamps lit the street. From somewhere nearby a horse trotted past. A couple of children were playing around one of the lamps. Jherek and Mr Wells turned a corner.

'This is the High Street,' Mr Wells informed him. 'I was born here, you know. It hasn't changed that much, though Bromley itself has expanded. It's pretty much a suburb of London now.'

'Ah,' murmured Jherek.

'There's Medhurst's,' Mr Wells pointed towards a darkened shop-front, 'and that's where Atlas House used to be. It was never much of a success, my father's china shop. There's the old *Bell*, where most of the profits were spent. Cooper's the tailors, seems to have gone out of business.

Woodall's fish-shop...' He chuckled. 'For a time, you know, this was Heaven for me. Then it was Hell. Now, it's merely Purgatory.'

'Why have you come back, Mr Wells?'

'Business of my father's to clear up. I'll stop at the *Rose and Crown* and go back in the morning. It doesn't do any harm for a writer to take a look at his roots occasionally. I've come a long way since Bromley and Up Park. I've been very lucky, I suppose.'

'And so have I been lucky, Mr Wells, in meeting you.' Jherek was almost ecstatic. 'Bromley!' he breathed.

'You must be this town's first tourist, Mr Carnelian.'

'Thank you,' Jherek said vaguely.

'Now,' said Mr Wells, 'I'll put you on your way to Collins Avenue, then I'll head for the *Rose and Crown* before they begin to wonder what's happened to me.'

Mr Wells escorted him through several streets, where the hedges were extremely high and the houses much newer looking, until they paused on a corner of one tree-lined, gas-lit road. 'Here we are in darkest semi-detached land,' Mr Wells announced. 'Collins Avenue, see?'

He pointed out a sign which Jherek couldn't read.

'And where would Number Twenty Three be?'

'Well, I'd say about half-way up – let's see – on this side of the road. Yes – can you see it – right by that lamp.'

'You're very kind, Mr Wells. In a few moments I shall be re-united with my lost love! I have crossed thousands of centuries to be at her side! I have disproved the Morphail Theorem! I have dared the dangerous and surging seas of Time! At last, at last, I near the end of my arduous quest for Bromley!' Jherek took Mr Wells by the shoulders and kissed him firmly upon the forehead. 'And it is thanks to *you*, Mr Wells, my dear!'

Mr Wells backed away, perhaps a trifle nervously. 'Glad to have been of insistence – um – assistance to you, Mr Carnelian. Now I really must rush.' And he turned and began to walk rapidly back in the direction they had come from.

Jherek was too happy to notice any change in Mr Wells's manner. He strode with buoyant steps along the pavement of Collins Avenue. He reached a gate of curly cast iron. He jumped over it and walked up a crazy-paving path to the door of a red-brick Gothic villa not at all unlike the one Mrs Underwood had had him build for her at the End of Time.

He knew what to do, for she had trained him well. He found the bell. He tugged it. He removed his top hat, wishing that he had remembered to bring some flowers with him. He studied, in admiration, the stained glass lilies set into the top half of the door.

There came a movement from within the house and at last the door was opened, but not by Mrs Underwood. A rather young girl stood there. She wore black, with a white cap and a white apron. She looked at Jherek Carnelian with a mixture of surprise, curiosity and contempt.

'Yus?'

'This is Twenty Three Collins Avenue, Bromley, Kent, England, 1896?'

'It is.'

'The residence of the beautiful Mrs Amelia Underwood?'

'It's the Underwood residence right enough. What's your business?'

'I have come to see Mrs Underwood. Is she within?'

'What's the name?'

'Carnelian. Tell her that Jherek Carnelian is here to take her back to their love-nest.'

'Gor blimey!' said the young girl. 'It's a bloomin' loony!'

'I do not follow you.'

'You'd better not try, mister. Be off wiv yer! Garn! Mrs Underwood'll 'ave the p'lice on yer wiv talk like that!' She tried to close the door, but Jherek was already partly inside. 'Mrs Underwood's a respectable lady! Shove off – go *on*!'

'I am really at a loss,' said Jherek mildly, 'to understand why you should have become so excited.' Baffled, he still refused to budge. 'Please tell Mrs Underwood that I am here.'

'Oh, lor! Oh, lor!' cried the girl. ''Ave a bit o' sense, will yer! You'll get yerself arrested! There's a good chap – be on yer way and we'll say no more abart it.'

'I have come for Mrs Underwood,' Jherek said firmly. 'I don't know why you should wish to stop me from seeing her. Perhaps I have offended one of your customs? I was convinced that I had done everything right. If there is something I should do – some convention I should follow – point it out, point it out. I have no desire to be rude.'

'Rude! Oh, lor!' And turning her head she shouted back into the hall. 'Mum! Mum! There's a maniac outside. I can't 'old him all be meself!'

A door opened. The hallway grew lighter. A figure in a dress of maroon velvet appeared.

'Mrs Underwood!' cried Jherek. 'Mrs Amelia Underwood! It is I, Jherek Carnelian, returned to claim you for my own!'

Mrs Underwood was as beautiful as ever, but even as he watched she grew gradually paler and paler. She leaned against the wall, her hand rising to her face. Her lips moved, but no sound issued from them.

'Help me, mum!' begged the maid, retreating into the hall. 'I can't manage 'im be meself. You know 'ow strong these loonies can be!'

'I have returned, Mrs Underwood. I have returned!'

'You—' He could barely hear the words. 'You – were *hanged*, Mr Carnelian. By the neck, until dead.'

'Hanged? In the time machine, you mean? I thought you said you would go with me. I waited. You were evidently unable to join me. So I came back.'

'C-came back!'

He pushed his way past the shivering maid. He stretched out his arms to embrace the woman he loved.

She put a pale hand to a pale forehead. There was a certain wild, distracted look in her eyes and she seemed to be talking to herself.

'My experiences – too much – knew I had not recovered properly – brain fever...'

And before he could take her to him she had collapsed upon the red and black Moorish-patterned carpet.

CHAPTER TWELVE

THE AWFUL DILEMMA OF MRS AMELIA UNDERWOOD

'*Now* look wot you've gorn an' done!' said the little maid accusingly. 'Ain't you ashamed of yerself?'

'How could I have made her swoon?'

'You frightened 'er somefink crool – jest like you frightened *me*! All that dirty talk!'

Jherek kneeled beside Mrs Amelia Underwood, patting ineffectually at her limp hands.

'You promise you won't do nuffink *nasty* an' I'll go an' get some water an' *sal volatile*,' said the girl, looking at him warily.

'Nasty? I?'

'Oo, yore a cool one!' The girl's tone was half-chiding,

half-admiring as she left the hall through a door under the staircase, but she no longer seemed to regard him as a complete menace. She returned very quickly, holding a glass of water in one hand and a small green bottle in the other. 'Stand back,' she said firmly. She joined Jherek on the floor, lifted Mrs Underwod's head under one arm and put the bottle to her nose. Mrs Underwood moaned.

'Yore very lucky indeed,' the maid said, 'that Mr Underwood's at 'is meeting. But 'e'll be back soon enough. *Then* you'll be in trouble!'

Mrs Underwood opened her eyes. When she saw Jherek, she closed them again. And again she moaned, but this time it seemed that she moaned with despair.

'Have no fear,' whispered Jherek. 'I will have you away from all this as soon as you have recovered.'

Her voice, when she managed to speak, was quite controlled. 'Where have you been, Mr Carnelian, if you were not hanged?'

'Been? In my own age, of course. The age you love. Where we were happy.'

'I am happy *here*, Mr Carnelian, with my husband, Mr Underwood.'

'Of course. But you are not as happy as you would be with me.'

She took a sip from the glass of water, brushed the smelling salts aside, and began to get to her feet. Jherek and the maid helped her. She walked slowly into the sitting room, a rather understated version of the one Jherek had created for her. The harmonium, he noticed, did not have nearly so many stops as the one he had made, and the aspidistra was not as vibrant; neither was the quality of the antimacassars all it could have been. But the smell was better. It was fuller, staler.

Carefully she seated herself in one of the large armchairs near the fireplace. Jherek remained standing. She said to the girl:

'You may go, Maude Emily.'

'Go, miss?'

'Yes, dear. Mr Carnelian, though a stranger to our customs, is not dangerous. He is from abroad.'

'Aeow!' said Maude Emily, considerably relieved and illumined, satisfied now that she had an explanation which covered everything. 'Well, I'm sorry about the mistake then, sir.' She made something of a curtsey and left.

'She's a good-hearted girl, but not very well trained,' said Mrs Underwood apologetically. 'You know the difficulties one has getting – but, of course, you would not know. She has only been with us a fortnight and has broken almost every scrap of china in the house, but she means well. We got her from a Home, you know.'

'A home?'

'A Home. A Girl's Home. Something like a Reformatory. The idea is not to punish them but to train them for some useful occupation in Life. Usually, of course, they go into Service.'

The word had a faintly familiar ring to it. 'Cannon fodder!' said Jherek. 'A shilling a day!' He felt at something of a loss.

'I had forgotten,' she said. 'Forgive me. You know so little about our society.'

'On the contrary,' he said. 'I know even more than before. When we return, Mrs Underwood, you will be surprised at how much I have learned.'

'I do not intend to return to your decadent age, Mr Carnelian.'

There was an icy quality in her voice which he found disturbing.

'I was only too happy to escape,' she continued. Then, a little more kindly, 'Not, of course, that you weren't the soul of hospitality, after your fashion. I shall always be grateful to you for that, Mr Carnelian. I had begun to convince myself that I had dreamed most of what took place...'

'Dreamed that you loved me?'

'I did not tell you I loved you, Mr Carnelian.'

'You indicated...'

'You misread my—'

'I cannot read at all. I thought you would teach me.'

'I mean that you misinterpreted something I might have said. I was not myself, that time in the garden. It was fortunate that I was snatched away before we ... Before we did anything we should both regret.'

He was not perturbed. 'You love me. I know you do. In your letter—'

'I love Mr Underwood. He is my husband.'

'I shall be your husband.'

'It is not possible.'

'Anything is possible. When I return, my power rings...'

'It is not what I meant, Mr Carnelian.'

'We could have real children,' he said coaxingly.

'Mr Carnelian!' Her colour had returned at last.

'You are beautiful,' he said.

'Please, Mr Carnelian.'

He sighed with pleasure. 'Very beautiful.'

'I shall have to ask you to leave. As it is, my husband will be returning shortly, from his meeting. I shall have to explain that you are an old friend of my father's – that he met your family when he was a missionary in the South Seas. It will be a lie, and I hate to lie. But it will save both our feelings. Say as little as possible.'

'You know that you love me,' he announced firmly. 'Tell him that. You will leave with me now.'

'I will do no such thing! Already there has been difficulty – my appearance in court – the potential scandal. Mr Underwood is not an over-imaginative man, but he became quite suspicious at one point...'

'Suspicious?'

'Of the story I was forced to concoct, to try to save you, Mr Carnelian, from the noose.'

'Noose of what?'

A note of desperation entered her voice. 'How, by the way, did you manage to escape death and come here?'

'I did not know death threatened! I suppose it is always a risk in time travel, though. I came here thanks to the help of a kindly, mechanical old creature called Nurse. I had been trying for some while to find a means of returning to 1896 so that we might be reunited. A happy accident led to a succession of events which finally resulted in my arrival here, in Collins Avenue. Do you know a Mr Wells?'

'No. Did he claim to know me?'

'No. He was on some business of his father's at the *Rose and Crown*. He was telling me that he invented time machines. A hobby, I gather. He does not manufacture them, but leaves that to others. I had meant to ask him for the name of a craftsman who could build one for us. It will make our return much easier.'

'Mr Carnelian, I *have* returned – for good. This is my home.'

He looked critically about him. 'It is smaller than *our* home. It has a trace or two more authenticity, I'll grant you, but it lacks a certain life, wouldn't you say? Perhaps I should not mention Mr Underwood's failings, but it would seem to me he could have given you a little more.' He lost interest in the subject and began to feel in his pockets, to see if he had brought something which could be a gift, but all he had was the deceptor-gun Nurse had handed back to him shortly before he had begun his journey. 'I know that you like bunches of flowers and water closets and so forth (you see, I have remembered every detail of what you told me) but I forgot to make some flowers, and a water closet, of course, might have proved too bulky an object to carry through time. However,' and he had a revelation as he began to tug off his nicest power ring, a ruby, 'if you would accept this, I would be more than happy.'

'I cannot accept gifts of any sort from you, Mr Carnelian. How should I explain it to my husband?'

'Explain that I had given you something? Would that be necessary?'

'Oh, please, please go!' She started as she heard a movement in the passage outside. 'It is he!' She stared wildly around the room. 'Remember,' she said in an urgent whisper, 'what I told you.'

'I will try, but I don't understand...'

The door of the sitting room opened and a man of average height entered.

Mr Underwood wore a pair of pince-nez upon his nose. His hay-coloured hair was parted firmly in the middle. His high, white collar pressed mercilessly into his pink neck and the knot of his tie was so tight and small as to be almost microscopic. He was unbuttoning his jacket with the air of a man removing protective clothing in an environment which might not be altogether safe. Precisely, he put down a black book he had carried in with him. Precisely, he raised his eyebrows and, with precision, brushed back a hair which had strayed loose from his perfectly symmetrical moustache. 'Good evening,' he said, with only a hint of enquiry. He acknowledged the presence of his wife. 'My dear.'

'Good evening, Harold. Harold, this is Mr Carnelian. He has just come from the Antipodes, where his father and mine, as you might recall, were missionaries.'

'Carnelian? An unusual name, sir. Yet, as I remember, the same as that felon's who...'

'His brother,' said Mrs Underwood. 'I was commiserating with him as you entered.'

'A dreadful business,' Mr Underwood glanced at a newspaper on the sideboard with the eye of a hunter who sees his quarry disappearing from bowshot. He sighed and perhaps he smiled. 'My wife was very brave, you know, in offering to speak for the defence. Great risk of scandal. I was only telling Mr Griggs, at the Bible Meeting tonight, that if we all had such courage in following the teachings of our conscience we might come considerably closer to the gates of the Kingdom of Heaven.'

'Ha, ha,' said Mrs Underwood. 'You are very kind, Harold. I only did my duty.'

'We do not all have your fortitude, my dear. She is an admirable woman, is she not, Mr Carnelian?'

'Without doubt,' said Jherek feelingly. He stared with unashamed curiosity at his rival. 'The most wonderful woman in your world – in any world, Mr Underwood.'

'Um, yes,' said Mr Underwood. 'You are, of course, grateful for the sacrifice she made. Your enthusiasm is understandable...'

'Sacrifice?' Jherek turned to Mrs Underwood. 'I was not aware that this society practised such rites? Whom did you...?'

'You have been away from England a long time, sir?' asked Mr Underwood.

'This is my second visit,' Jherek told him.

'Aha!' Mr Underwood seemed satisfied by the explanation. 'In the darkest depths of the jungle, eh? Bringing light to the savage mind.'

'I was in a forest...' said Jherek.

'He only recently heard of his brother's sad fate,' broke in Mrs Underwood.

Jherek could not understand why she kept interrupting them. He felt he was getting on quite well with Mr Underwood; getting on rather better, in truth, than he had expected.

'Have you offered Mr Carnelian some refreshment, my dear?' Mr Underwood's pince-nez glinted as he looked about the room. 'We are, needless to say, teetotallers here, Mr Carnelian. But if you would care for some tea...?'

Mrs Underwood pulled enthusiastically at a bell-rope. 'What a good idea!' she cried.

Maude Emily appeared almost immediately and was instructed to bring tea and biscuits for the three of them. She looked from Mr Underwood to Jherek Carnelian and back again. The look was significant and caused the faintest expression of panic in Mrs Underwood's otherwise resolutely set features.

'Tea!' said Jherek as Maude Emily left. 'I don't believe I've ever had it. Or did we—'

This time, inadvertently, Mr Underwood came to his wife's rescue. 'Never had tea, what? Oh, then this is a treat you cannot miss! You must spend most of your time away from civilization, Mr Carnelian.'

'From this one, yes.'

Mr Underwood removed his pince-nez. From his pocket he took a large, white handkerchief. He polished the pince-nez. 'I take your meaning, sir,' he said gravely. 'Who are we to accuse the poor savage of his lack of culture, when we live in such Godless times ourselves?'

'Godless? I was under the impression that this was a Religious Age.'

'Mr Carnelian, you are misinformed, I fear. Your faith is allowed to blossom unchecked, no doubt, as you sit in some far-off native hut, with only your Bible and Our Lord for company. But the distractions one has to contend with in this England of ours are enough to make one give up altogether and look to the consolations of the High Church. Why,' his voice dropped, 'I knew a man, a resident of Bromley, who came very close once to turning towards *Rome*.'

'He could not find Bromley?' Jherek laughed, glad that he and Mr Underwood were getting on so well. 'I had a great deal of trouble myself. If I had not met a Mr Wells at a place called, as I remember, the Café Royale, I should still be looking for it!'

'*The Café Royale!*' hissed Mr Underwood, in much the same tone as he had said 'Rome'. He replaced his pince-nez and stared hard at Jherek Carnelian.

'I had become lost...' Jherek began to explain.

'Who has not, before he enters the door of that gateway to the underworld?'

'... and met someone who had lived in Bromley.'

'No longer, I trust?'

'So I gathered.'

Mr Underwood breathed a sigh of relief. 'Mr Carnelian,' he said, 'you would do well to remember the fate of your poor brother. Doubtless he was as innocent as you when he first came to London. I beg you to remember that not for nothing has it been called Satan's Own City!'

'Who would this Mr Satan be?' asked Jherek conversationally. 'You see, I was re-creating the city and it would be useful to have the advice of one who...'

'Maude Emily!' sang Mrs Underwood, as if greeting the sight of land after many days in an open boat. 'The tea!' She turned to them. 'The tea is here!'

'Ah, the tea,' said Mr Underwood, but he was frowning as he mulled over Jherek's latest words. Even Jherek had the idea that he had somehow said the wrong thing, in spite of being so careful – not that he felt there was very much point in Mrs Underwood's deception. All he needed to do, really, was to explain the problem to Mr Underwood (who plainly did not share his passion for Mrs Underwood) and Mr Underwood would accept that he, Jherek, was likely to be far happier with Mrs Underwood. Mr Underwood could remain here (with Maude Emily, perhaps) and Mrs Underwood would leave with him, Jherek.

As Maude Emily poured the tea and Mrs Underwood stood near the fireplace fiddling with a small lace handkerchief and Mr Underwood peered through his pince-nez as if to make sure that Maude Emily poured the correct amount of tea into each cup, Jherek said:

'I expect you are happy here, aren't you, Maude Emily, with Mr Underwood?'

'Yes, sir,' she said in a small voice.

'And you are happy with Maude Emily, Mr Underwood?'

Mr Underwood waved a hand and moved his lips, indicating that he was as happy with her as he felt he had to be.

'Splendid,' said Jherek.

A silence followed. He was handed a tea-cup.

'What do you think?' Mr Underwood had become quite animated as he watched Jherek sip. 'There are those who shun the use of tea, claiming that it is a stimulant we can well do without.' He smiled bleakly. 'But I'm afraid we should not be human if we did not have our little sins, eh? Is it good, Mr Carnelian?'

'Very nice,' said Jherek. 'Actually, I have had it before. But we called it something different. A longer name. What was it, Mrs Underwood.'

'How should I know, Mr Carnelian.' She spoke lightly, but she was glaring at him.

'Lap something,' said Jherek. 'Sou something.'

'Lap-san-sou-chong! Ah, yes. A great favourite of yours, my dear, is it not? China tea.'

'There!' said Jherek beaming by way of confirmation.

'You have met my wife before, Mr Carnelian?'

'As children,' said Mrs Underwood. 'I explained it to you, Harold.'

'You surely were not given tea to drink as children?'

'Of course not,' she replied.

'Children?' Jherek's mind had been on other things, but now he brightened. 'Children? Do you plan to have any children, Mr Underwood.'

'Unfortunately.' Mr Underwood cleared his throat. 'We have not so far been blessed...'

'Something wrong?'

'Ah, no...'

'Perhaps you haven't got the hang of making them by the straightforward old-fashioned method? I must admit it took me a while to work it out. You know,' Jherek turned to make sure that Mrs Underwood was included in the conversation, 'finding what goes in where and so forth!'

'Nnng,' said Mrs Underwood.

'Good heavens!' Mr Underwood still had his tea-cup poised half-way to his lips. For the first time, since he had entered the room, his eyes seemed to live.

Jherek's body shook with laughter. 'It involved a lot of research. My mother, the Iron Orchid, explained what she knew and, in the long run, when we had pooled the information, was able to give me quite a lot of practical experience. She has always been interested in new ideas for love-making. She told me that while genuine sperm had been used in my conception, otherwise the older method had not been adhered to. Once she got the thing worked out, however (and it involved some minor biological transformations) she told me that she had rarely enjoyed love-making in the conventional ways more. Is anything the matter, Mr Underwood? Mrs Underwood?'

'Sir,' said Mr Underwood, addressing Jherek with cool reluctance, 'I believe you to be mad. In charity, I must assume that you and your brother are cursed with that same disease of the brain which sent him to the gallows.'

'My brother?' Jherek frowned. Then he winked at Mrs Underwood. 'Oh, yes, my brother...'

Mrs Underwood, breathing heavily, sat down suddenly upon the rug, while Maude Emily had her lips together, had gone very red in the face, and was making strange, strangled noises.

'Why did you come here? Oh, why did you come here?' murmured Mrs Underwood from the floor.

'Because I love you, as you know,' explained Jherek patiently. 'You see, Mr Underwood,' he began confidentially, 'I wish to take Mrs Underwood away with me.'

'Indeed?' Mr Underwood presented to Jherek a peculiarly glassy and crooked grin. 'And what, might I ask, do you intend to offer my wife, Mr Carnelian?'

'Offer? Gifts? Yes, well,' again he felt in his pockets but again could find nothing but the deceptor-gun. He drew it out. 'This?'

Mr Underwood flung his hands into the air.

CHAPTER THIRTEEN

STRANGE EVENTS IN BROMLEY ONE NIGHT IN THE SUMMER OF 1896

'Spare them,' said Mr Underwood. 'Take me, if you must!'

'But I don't want you, Mr Underwood,' Jherek said reasonably, gesturing with the gun. 'Though it is kind of you to offer. It is *Mrs* Underwood I want. She loves me, you see, and I love her.'

'Is this true, Amelia?'

Dumbly, she shook her head.

'You have been conducting a liaison of some sort with this man?'

'That's the word I was trying to think of,' said Jherek.

'I don't believe you are that murderer's brother at all.'

Mr Underwood remembered to keep his hands firmly above his head. 'Somehow you have escaped the gallows – and you, Amelia, seem to have played a part in thwarting justice. I felt at the time ...'

'No, Harold. I have nothing to be ashamed of – or, at least, very little ... If I tried to explain what had happened to me one night, when ...'

'One night, yes? When?'

'I was abducted.'

'By this man?'

'No, that came later. Oh, dear! I told you nothing, Harold, because I knew it would be impossible for you to believe. It would have put a burden upon you that I knew you should not have to bear.'

'The burden of truth, Amelia, is always easier to bear than the burden of deceit.'

'I was carried into our world's most distant future. How, I cannot explain. There I met Mr Carnelian, who was kind to me. I did not expect ever to return here, but return I did – to the same moment in which I had left. I decided that I had had a particularly vivid dream. Then I learned of Mr Carnelian's appearance in our time – he was being tried for murder.'

'So he is the same man!'

'I felt it my duty to help him. I knew that he could not be guilty. I tried to prove that he was insane so that his life, at least, would be spared. My efforts, however, were fruitless. They were not helped by Mr Carnelian's naïve insistence upon a truth which none could be expected to believe. He was sentenced to death. The last I knew, he had perished through the usual auspices of the Law.'

'Preposterous,' said Mr Underwood. 'I can see that I have been an absolute fool. If you are not as mad as he, then you are guilty of the most unholy deception ever practised by an erring wife upon her trusting husband.' Mr Underwood was trembling. He ran a hand across his head, disturbing his hair. He loosened his tie. 'Well, luckily the Bible is very clear on such matters. You must go, of course. You must leave my house, Amelia, and thank Our Lord Jesus Christ for the New Testament and its counsels. If we lived in Old Testament times, your punishment would not be so lenient!'

'Harold, please. You are distraught, I can see. If you will try to listen to Mr Carnelian's story...'

'Ha! Must I listen to his ravings any further, before he kills me?'

'Kill you?' said Jherek mildly. 'Is that what you want, Mr Underwood? I'd willingly do anything to help...'

'Oh!'

Jherek saw Maude Emily leaving the room. Perhaps she had become so bored with the conversation. He was certainly having quite a lot of difficulty understanding Mr Underwood, whose voice was shaking so much, and pitched so high at times, that the words were distorted.

'I will do nothing to stand in your way,' Mr Underwood told him. 'Take her and leave, if that is what you want. She has told you she loves you?'

'Oh, yes. In a letter.'

'A letter! Amelia?'

'I wrote a letter, but...'

'So you are foolish, as well as treacherous. To think that, under my own roof, I supported such a creature. I had thought you upright. I had thought you a true Christian. Why, Amelia, I *admired* you. Admired you, it seems, for what was merely your disguise, a cloak of hypocrisy.'

'Oh, Harold, how can you believe such things? If you knew the lengths to which I went to defend my—'

'Honour? Really, my dear, you must consider me a pretty poor sort of brain, if you think you can continue any further with your charade!'

'Well,' said Jherek cheerfully, wishing that Mr Underwood would make his meaning clearer, but glad that the main problem had been cleared up, 'shall we be off, Mrs Underwood?'

'I cannot, Mr Carnelian. My husband is not himself. The shock of your appearance and of your – your language. I know that you do not mean badly, but the disruption you are causing is much worse than I feared. Mr Carnelian – please put the gun back in your pocket!'

He slipped it into its old place. 'I was going to offer it in exchange. As I understood...'

'You understand nothing at all, Mr Carnelian. It would be best if you left...'

'Leave with him, Amelia. I insist upon it.' Mr Underwood lowered his hands, drew out his pocket handkerchief and, with a precise, thoughtful air, glancing often at the white cloth, mopped his brow. 'It is what you both want, is it not? Your freedom. Oh, I gladly give it to you. You pollute the sanctity of my home!'

'Harold, I can scarcely believe the vehemence – you have always preached charity. You are normally so *calm*!'

'Should I be calm, now?'

'I suppose not, but...'

'All my life I have lived by certain principles – principles I understood you to share. Must I join you in throwing them aside? Your father, the Reverend Mr Vernon, once warned me that you were overly inclined to high spirits. When we married, I found no sign of that side of your character and assumed that the sober business of being a good wife had driven it from you. Instead, it was buried. And not very deeply, either!'

'I fear, Harold, that it is you who are mad!'

He turned his back on them. 'Go!'

'You will regret this, Harold. You know you will.'

'Regret my wife conducting a liaison under my own roof with a convicted murderer? Yes!' He laughed without humour. 'I suppose I shall!'

Jherek took Mrs Underwood's arm. 'Shall we be off?'

Her imploring eyes were still upon her husband, but she allowed Jherek to lead her to the door.

And then they were in the peace of Collins Avenue. Jherek realized that Mrs Underwood was disturbed by the parting.

'I think Mr Underwood accepted the situation very

well, don't you? There you are, you see, all your fears, Mrs Underwood, were groundless. The truth is always worth telling. Mr Underwood said as much. Perhaps he did not behave as gracefully as one might have hoped, but still...'

'Mr Carnelian, I know my husband. This behaviour is untypical, to say the least. You have been responsible for making him undergo greater strain than anyone should have to tolerate. I, too, am partly responsible...'

'Why are you speaking in a whisper, Mrs Underwood?'

'The neighbours.' She shook her head. 'We might as well walk a little, I suppose. It will give Harold time to think things over. These Bible Meetings of his sometimes take rather more out of him than one might expect. He is very dedicated. His people have been missionaries for generations. It was always his regret that he could not follow in his father's footsteps. His health, while not singularly poor, is badly affected by hot climates. He has been like it from a small child, his mother was telling me.' She checked her flow. 'I am babbling, I fear.'

'Babble on, beautiful Mrs Underwood!' Jherek's stride was light and long. 'We shall soon be where we both belong. I remember every word of the letter Mr Griffiths read to me. Particularly the last part: " – and so I must tell you, Jherek, that I do love you, that I miss you, that I shall always remember you." Oh, how happy I am. Now I know what happiness *is*!'

'Mr. Carnelian, I wrote that letter in haste.' She added resentfully, 'I thought you were about to die.'

'I can't understand why.'

A deep sigh escaped her and she did not explain further.

They walked through a number of streets very similar to Collins Avenue (Jherek wondered how the people could find their way to their individual dwellings) and after a while Jherek noticed that she was shivering. He, himself, had become conscious of an increased chill in the air. He removed his coat and put it around her shoulders.

She did not resist the gesture.

'Thank you,' she said. 'If I were not a sensible woman, Mr Carnelian, I might at this moment be thinking that I have been ruined. I prefer to think, however, that Harold will come to understand his error and that we may be reconciled.'

'He will live with Maude Emily,' Jherek told her. 'He indicated as much. She will comfort him.'

'Oh, dear. Oh, dear.' Mrs Underwood shook her head. The road had given way to a path which ran between first fences and then hedges. Beyond the hedges were open fields. The sky was clear and a large moon offered plenty of light.

'I think that we are probably going in the wrong direction for the *Rose and Crown.*'

'Why should you wish to visit a public house?'

'*Public* house?'

'Why do you want to go to the *Rose and Crown,* Mr Carnelian?'

'To see Mr Wells, of course, Mrs Underwood. To ask him the name of a good maker of time machines.'

'In my age, there are no such things as time machines. If this acquaintance of yours told you that, he was probably having some sort of joke with you.'

'Oh, no. Our conversation was most serious. He was one of the few people I have met in your world who seemed to know exactly what I was talking about.'

'He was doubtless humouring you. Where did this conversation take place?'

'On the train. And what a marvellous experience that was, in its own right. I shall be making plenty of modifications as soon as we return.'

'Then you have no means, as yet, of escaping to your original period?'

'Well, no, but I can't see any difficulty, really.'

'There could be difficulties for both of us if Maude Emily, as I suspect, went for a policeman. If my husband has not had time to calm down he will inform the policeman, when he arrives, that an escaped murderer and his female accomplice are even now in the vicinity of Bromley – and that the man is armed. What was that thing you were waving, anyway?'

'The deceptor-gun? Would you like me to demonstrate it?'

'I think not.'

From the distance the silence of the night was broken by the sound of a high-pitched whistling.

'The police!' gasped Mrs Underwood. 'It is as I feared.' She clutched his arm, then removed her hand almost immediately. 'If they find you, you are doomed!'

'Why so? You refer to the gentlemen with the helmets who helped me before. They will have access to a time machine. It was thanks to them, after all, that I was able to return to my own age on my previous visit.'

She ignored him, pushing him through a gate and into a field. It smelled sweet and he paused to take the scent into his lungs. 'There is no question,' he began, 'that I have much to learn. Smells, for instance, are generally missing in my reproductions, and when they do exist they lack subtlety. If there were only some way of recording ...'

'Silence!' she whispered urgently. 'See, they are coming this way.' She pointed back to the road. A number of small, dancing lights were in evidence. 'It is their bulls-eyes. The whole of the Bromley constabulary must be on your trail!'

Again a whistle sounded. They crouched behind the hedge, listening to the swish of bicycle tyres over the unmade road.

'They'll be making for the railway station, that's my guess,' said a gruff voice. 'They'd be fools to head for open countryside. We're on a wild-goose chase.'

'You can never be sure about madmen,' said another voice. 'I was part of the lot what tracked down the Lewisham Murderer three years ago. They found 'im cool as a cucumber in a boarding 'ouse not five streets away from the scene of the crime. 'E'd bin there for a fortnight, while we raced about half of Kent night and day catching nothing but colds in the 'ead.'

'I *still* think they'll try for a train. That bloke said 'e *came* on the train.'

'We're not entirely sure it was the same man. Besides, 'e said *two* men, obviously friends, got off the train. What 'appened to the other?'

'I don't believe 'e *did* come on the train.'

'What's 'e doin' in Bromley, any'ow?' said a third voice complainingly.

'Come back for 'is bit o' stuff – you know what some women're like – go 'ead over 'eels for that sort. I've seen it before – perficktly decent women brought low by a smooth-talking villain. If she ain't careful I'd say she'll be 'is next victim.'

'Often the way it goes,' another agreed.

They passed out of earshot. Mrs Underwood seemed to have a high colour again. 'Really!' she said. 'So I already have a reputation as the consort of criminals. Mud sticks, as they say. Well, Mr Carnelian, you will never understand the damage you have done, I know, but I am currently very much regretting that I allowed my better nature to take me to the Old Bailey in your defence! Even at the time, there was a hint of gossip – but now – well, I shall have to consider leaving the country. And poor Harold – why should he be made to suffer?'

'Leaving? Good.' He stood up, brushing pieces of straw from his trousers. 'Now, let's go and find Mr Wells.'

'Mr Carnelian – it is really far too dangerous. You heard those policemen. The station is being watched. They are combing Bromley for us!'

Jherek was still puzzled. 'If they wish to talk to us, why do we not let them? What harm can they do us?'

'Considerable harm, Mr Carnelian. Take my word for it.'

He shrugged. 'Very well, Mrs Underwood, I shall. However, there is still the question of Mr Wells...'

'I assure you, also, that this Mr Wells of yours can be

nothing but a charlatan. Time machines do not exist in this century.'

'I believe he has written a book on them.'

Understanding dawned. She frowned. 'There *was* a book. I read about it last year. A fantasy. Fiction. It was nothing but fiction!'

'What is "fiction"?'

'A made-up story – about things which are not real.'

'Everything, surely, is *real*?'

'About things which do not exist...' She was labouring, trying to find the right words.

'But time machines *do* exist. You know that, Mrs Underwood, as well as I do!'

'Not yet,' she said. 'Not in 1896.'

'Mr Wells suggested otherwise. Who am I to believe?'

'You love me?'

'You know that I do.'

'Then believe *me*,' she said firmly, and she took his hand and led him across the field.

Some time later, they lay in a dry ditch, looking at the outline of a building Mrs Underwood had described as a farmhouse. Once or twice they had seen the lights of the policemen's lanterns some way off, but now it seemed their pursuers had lost the trail. Jherek was still not entirely convinced that Mrs Underwood had interpreted the situation correctly.

'I distinctly heard one of them say they were looking for geese,' he informed her. She seemed tired from all the running about and her eyes kept closing as she tried to find a more comfortable position in the ditch. 'Geese, and not people.'

'We must get the assistance of some influential man, who will take up your case, perhaps be able to convince the authorities of the truth.' She had pointedly ignored almost all his comments since they had left the house. 'I wonder – this Mr Wells is a writer. You mentioned his reference to the *Saturday Review*? That is quite a respectable journal – or at least it used to be. I haven't seen a copy for some time. If he could publish something – or if he has friends in the legal profession. Possibly it would be a good idea to try to see him, after all. If we hide in that barn during the night and leave early in the morning, we might be able to get to him after the police have decided we have made our escape.'

Wearily, she rose. 'Come along, Mr Carnelian.' She began to tramp across the field towards the barn.

In approaching the barn, they had to pass close to the farmyard and now several dogs began to bark excitedly. An upper window was flung open, a lantern blazed, a deep voice called: 'Who is it? What is it?'

'Good evening to you,' cried Jherek. Mrs Underwood tried to cover his mouth with her hand but it was too late. 'We are out for a stroll, sampling the joys of your countryside. I must congratulate you...'

'By cracky, it's the lunatic!' explained the unseen man. 'The one we were warned was on the loose. I'll get my gun!'

'Oh, this is unbearable!' wept Mrs Underwood. 'And look!'

Three or four lights could be seen in the distance.

'The police?'

'Without doubt.'

From the farmhouse came a great banging about, shouts and barkings, and lights appeared downstairs. Mrs Underwood grabbed Jherek by the sleeve and drew him inside the first building. In the darkness something snorted and stamped.

'It's a horse!' said Jherek. 'They always delight me and I have seen so many now.'

Mrs Underwood was speaking to the horse, stroking its nose, murmuring to it. It became calmer.

From the farmyard there was a sudden report and the deep-voiced man yelled: 'Oh, damn! I've shot the pig!'

'We have one chance of escape now,' said Mrs Underwood, flinging a blanket over the horse's back. 'Pass me that saddle, Mr Carnelian, and hurry.'

He did not know what a 'saddle' was, but he gathered it must be a strange contraption made out of leather and brass which hung on the wall near to his head. It was heavy. As best he could, he helped her put it on the horse's back. Expertly she tightened straps and passed a ribbon of leather around the beast's head. He watched admiringly.

'Now,' she hissed, 'quickly. Mount.'

'Is this the proper time for such things, do you think'?

'Climb onto the horse, and then help me up.'

'I have no idea how...'

She showed him. 'Put your foot in this. I'll steady the animal. Fling your leg over the saddle, find the other stirrup – that's this – and take hold of the reins. We have no alternative.'

'Very well. This is great fun, Mrs Underwood. I am glad that your sense of pleasure is returning.'

Climbing onto the horse was much harder than he would have thought, but eventually, just as another shot rang out, he was sitting astride the beast, his feet in the appropriate metal loops. Hitching up her skirts, Mrs Underwood managed to seat herself neatly across the saddle. She took the reins, saying to him 'Hang on to me!' and then the horse was trotting swiftly out of its stall and into the yard.

'By golly, they've got the 'orse!' cried the farmer. He raised his gun, but could not fire. Plainly he was not going to risk a horse as well as a pig in his bid to nail the madman.

At that moment about half-a-dozen burly policemen came rushing through the gate and all began to grab for the reins of the horse while Jherek laughed and Mrs Underwood tugged sharply at the reins crying, 'Your heels, Mr Carnelian. Use your heels!'

'I'm sorry, Mrs Underwood, I'm not sure what you mean!' Jherek was almost helpless with laughter now.

Frightened by the desperate police officers, the horse reared once, whinnied twice, rolled its eyes, jumped the fence and was off at a gallop.

The last Jherek Carnelian heard of those particular policemen was: 'Such goings on in Bromley! Who'd a credited it!'

There was the sound of a third shot, but it did not seem aimed at them and Jherek thought that probably the farmer and one of the police officers had collided in the dark.

Mrs Underwood was shouting at him. 'Mr Carnelian! You will have to try to help. I have lost control!'

With one hand on the saddle and the other about her waist, Jherek smiled happily as he was jolted mightily up and down; he came close to losing his seat upon the back of the beast. 'Ah, Mrs Underwood, I am delighted to hear it. At last!'

CHAPTER FOURTEEN

A SCARCITY OF TIME MACHINES

A fresh dawn brightened Bromley. Taking his leave of the *Rose and Crown*, having risen early to complete his business and be as swiftly as possible on his way, Mr Wells entered the High Street with the air of a man who had, during the night, wrestled with a devil and thoroughly conquered it. This return to Bromley had been reluctant for two reasons; the first reason being his own identification of the place with everything unimaginative, repressive and stultifying about England; the second was that his business was embarrassing in that he came as something of a petitioner, to save his father from an appearance in the County Court by clearing up a small financial matter which had, for many months, apparently escaped his father's attention. It was because of this that he had not been able to condescend to Bromley quite as much as he would have liked – after all, these were his roots. His father, as far as Bromley was concerned, had been a Failure, but the son was now on his way to being a Great Success, with five books already published and several more due to appear soon. He would have preferred his return to have been greeted with more publicity – perhaps a brief interview in the *Bromley Record* – and to have arrived in greater style, but the nature of his business made that impossible. Indeed, he hoped that nobody would recognize him and that was his main reason for leaving the hostelry so early. And the reason for his air of self-congratulation – he felt he was On Top of Bromley. It held no further fears for him. Questions of minor debts, of petty scandals, could no longer plunge him into the depths of anxiety he had once known. He had escaped from Bromley and now, by returning, he had escaped from the ghosts he had taken with him.

Mr Wells gave his stick a twirl. He gave his small moustache a flick (it had never grown quite as thick as he had hoped it would) and he pursed his lips in a silent whistle. A great sense of well-being filled him and he looked with a haughty eye upon Bromley; at the milkman's float with its ancient horse dragging it slowly along, at the newspaper delivery boy as he cycled from door to door, doubtless blessing the dull inhabitants of this dull town with news of dull civic doings, at the blinds still closed over all the familiar shop windows, including the window of Atlas House where his mother and father, intermittently, had brought him up and where his mother had done her best to instill in him the basic principles of Remaining Respectable.

He grinned. These days, he didn't give a fig for their Respectability. He was his own man, making his own way, according to his own rules. And what different rules they were! His encounter on the previous evening, with that strange, foreign young man, had cheered him up quite a bit, now realized. Thinking over their conversation, it had occurred to him that *The Time Machine* had been taken for literal truth by the stranger. That, surely, was a Sign of Success, if nothing was!

Birds sang, milk-cans clinked, the sky above the rooftops of Bromley was clear and blue, there was a fresh sort of smell in the air, a sense of peace. Mr Wells filled his lungs.

He expelled his breath slowly, alert and curious, now, to a new sound, a rather less peaceful sound, in the distance. He paused, expectantly, and then was astonished to see, rounding the bend in the High Street, a large plough-horse, lathered in sweat, foaming a little at the mouth, eyes rolling, galloping at full tilt in his direction. He stopped altogether as he saw that the horse had two riders, neither, it seemed, very securely mounted. In the front was a beautiful young woman in a maroon velvet dress covered in bits of straw, mud and leaves, her dark red curls in disarray. And behind her, with one hand about her waist, the other upon the reins, in his shirt-sleeves (his coat seemed to have slipped down between them and was flapping like an extra leg against the horse's side) was the young stranger, Mr Carnelian, whooping and laughing, for all the world like a stock-broker's clerk enjoying the fun of the roundabout ride at a Bank Holiday Fair. Its way partly blocked by the milk-man's float, the horse balked for a moment, and Mr Carnelian spotted Mr Wells. He waved cheerfully, lurching backwards and barely managing to recover his balance.

'Mr Wells! We were hoping to see you.'

Mr Wells's reply fell a little flat, even to his own ears: 'Well, here I am!'

'I was wondering if you knew who could make me a time machine?'

Mr Wells did his best to humour the foreigner and with a chuckle pointed with his stick to the bicycle supported in the hands of the gaping delivery boy. 'I'm afraid the nearest thing you'll find to a Time Machine hereabouts is that piece of ironmongery over there!'

Mr Carnelian took note of the bicycle and seemed ready to dismount, but then the horse was off again, with the young woman crying 'Woe! Woe!' or possibly 'Woah! Woah!' and her co-rider calling back over his shoulder: 'I am much obliged, Mr Wells! Thank you!'

Now five mud-drenched police constables on equally muddy cycles came racing round the corner and the leading officer was pointing at the disappearing pair, shouting: 'Collar 'im! It's the Mayfair Killer!'

Mr Wells watched in silence as the squadron went past, then he crossed the road to where the delivery boy was still standing, his jaw threatening to detach itself altogether from the rest of his face. Feeling in his waistcoat pocket, Mr Wells produced a coin. 'Would you care to sell me one of your papers?' he asked.

He had begun to wonder if Bromley had not ceased to be quite as dull as he remembered it.

Jherek Carnelian, with a bemused expression on his face, watched the oar drift away through the weed-strewn waters of the river. Mrs Underwood lay in fitful slumber at the other end of the boat (which they had requisitioned after the horse, on attempting to jump a fence a good ten miles from Bromley, had deposited them near the river).

Jherek had not had a great deal of success with the oars, anyway, and he was scarcely sorry to see the last one go. He leaned back, with one arm upon the tiller, and yawned. The day was extremely warm now and the sun was high in the sky. There came the lazy sounds of bees in the tall grass of the nearest bank and, on the other side of the river, white-clad ladies played croquet on a green and perfect lawn; the music of their tinkling laughter, the clack of mallets against balls, came faintly to Jherek's ears. This world was so *rich*, he thought, plucking a couple of small leaves off his battered jacket and inspecting them carefully. The texture, the detail, were all fascinating, and he wondered at the possibility of reproducing them when he and Mrs Underwood returned home.

Mrs Underwood stirred, rubbing at her eyes. 'Ah,' she said, 'I feel a little better for that.' She became aware of her surroundings. 'Oh, dear. We are adrift!'

'I lost the oars,' Jherek explained. 'See – there's one. But the current seems adequate. We are moving.'

She did not comment on this, but her lips curved in a smile which might have been described as philosophical rather than humorous.

'These time machines are much more common than you thought,' Jherek told her. 'I've seen several from the boat. People were riding them along the path beside the river. And those policemen had them, too. Probably thought they would follow us through Time.'

'Those are bicycles,' said Mrs Underwood.

'It's hard to tell them apart, I suppose. They all look very similar to me, but to your eye...'

'Bicycles,' she repeated, but without vehemence.

'Well,' he said, 'it all goes to show that your fears were groundless. We'll be back soon, you see.'

'Not by this method, I trust. In which direction are we heading?' She looked around her. 'Roughly westwards, I would say. We might easily be in Surrey. Ah, well, the police will find us eventually. I am reconciled.'

'In a world where Time seems so important,' Jherek mused, 'you'd think they would have more machines for manipulating it.'

'Time manipulates *us* in this world, Mr Carnelian.'

'As, of course, it will, according to Morphail. You see the reason I came so urgently to find you, Mrs Underwood, was that sooner or later we shall be plunged into the future, but the difference will be that we shall not be able to control our flight – we could land anywhere – we could be separated again.'

'I do not quite follow you, Mr Carnelian.' She dangled her hand in the water in a gesture which, for her, was almost abandoned.

'Once you have travelled into the future, you cannot remain for long in the past, lest a paradox result. Thus time itself ejects those whose presence in certain ages would lead to confusion, an alteration of history or something like that. How we have managed to remain so long in this period is a mystery. Presumably we have not yet begun to produce dangerous paradoxes. But I think that the moment we do, then we shall be on our way.'

'Are you suggesting that we shall have no choice?'

'I am. Thus we must make all speed to get back to *my* time, where you'll be happy. Admittedly, if we go into a future where time machines are less scarce, we should be able to make the journey in, as it were, several hops, but some of the periods between 1896 and the End of Time were exceptionally uncongenial and we could easily land in one of those.'

'You are trying to convince me, then, that I have no alternative?'

'It is the truth.'

'I have never known you to lie, Mr Carnelian.' She smiled that same smile again. 'I have often prayed that you would! Yet if I had remained in my own time and said nothing of what had happened to me, refused to act according to what I knew of the future, I might have remained here forever.'

'I suppose so. It might explain the instinct of some time travellers to speak as little of the future as possible and never to make use of their information. I have heard of these and it could be that they are "allowed" by Time to stay where they wish. By and large, however, few can resist talking of their adventures, making use of their information. Of course, we wouldn't really know about the ones who said nothing, would we? That could explain the flaw in the Morphail Theorem.'

'So – I shall say nothing and remain in 1896,' she said.

'By now Harold might have recovered his senses and if I tell the police that I was kidnapped by you I might not be charged as your accomplice. Moreover, if you disappear, then they'll never be able to prove you were the Mayfair Killer, somehow escaped from death. But we shall still need help.' She frowned.

There came a scraping sound from beneath them.

'Aha!' she said. 'We are in luck. The boat has run aground.'

They disembarked onto a narrow, sandy path. From the path ran a steep bank on which grew a variety of yellow, blue and scarlet flowers. At the top of the bank was a white fence.

While Mrs Underwood tidied her hair, using the river as a mirror, Jherek began to pick the flowers until he had quite a large bunch. His pursuit of a particularly fine specimen forced him to climb to the top of the bank so that he could then see what lay beyond the fence.

The bank went down to fields which were of a glowing green and oddly flat; and on the other side of the fields were a group of red-brick buildings, decorated with a number of rococo motifs in iron and stone. A tributary of the river ran alongside the buildings and in some of the more distant fields there were machines at work. The machines consisted of a heavy central cylinder from which extended about ten very long rods. As Jherek watched, the cylinders turned and the rods swung with them, distributing liquid evenly over the bright green fields. They were plainly agricultural robot workers; Jherek dimly remembered hearing about them in some malfunctioning record found in one of the rotted cities. He recalled that they had existed during the time of the Multitude Cultures, but he now knew enough about this particular period to be aware that they were still a rarity. This must then be something of an experimental project, he guessed. As such the buildings he could see could quite easily comprise a scientific establishment and, if so, there would be people there who would know how to go about procuring a time machine.

He was excited as he ran back down the bank, but he did not forget his priorities. He paused to arrange the flowers and, when she stood up from her toilet, turning towards him, he presented the bunch.

'A little late, I fear,' he said. 'But here they are! Your flowers, Mrs Underwood.'

She hesitated for a moment and then reached out to take them. 'Thank you, Mr Carnelian.' Her lips trembled.

He looked searchingly at her face. 'Your eyes –' he said – 'they seem wet. Did you splash some water into your face?'

She cleared her throat and put fingers first to one eye and then the other. 'I suppose I did,' she agreed.

'I believe that we are a little closer to our goal,' he told her, pointing back up the bank. 'It will not be long now before we are back in my own age and you can take up my "moral education" where you were forced to leave it, when you were snatched from my arms.'

She shook her head and her smile, now, seemed a little warmer. 'I sometimes wonder if you are *deliberately* naïve, Mr Carnelian. I have told you – my duty is to return to Harold and try to ease his mind. Think of him! He is not – not a flexible man. He must be in agony at this moment.'

'Well, if you wish to return, we will both go. I will explain to him in more detail...'

'That would not help. Somehow we must ensure your safety, then I will go to him on my own.'

'And after that, you will come to me?'

'No, Mr Carnelian.'

'Even though you love me?'

'Yes, Mr Carnelian. And, I say again. I have not confirmed what I said at a time when I was not altogether in my right senses. Besides, Mr Carnelian, what if I did love you? I have seen your world – your people play at real life – your emotions are the emotions of actors – sincere for the moment that they are displayed on stage before the public. Knowing this, how would I feel if I did love you? I would be aware that your love for me is nothing but a sentimental imposture, pursued, admittedly, with a certain persistence, but an imposture none the less.'

'Oh, no, no, no!' His large eyes clouded. 'How could you think that?'

They stood in silence upon the bank of the tranquil river. Her eyes were downcast as she looked at the flowers; her delicate hands stroked the petals; she breathed rapidly. He took a step towards her and then stopped. He thought for a moment, before he spoke.

'Mrs Underwood?'

'Yes, Mr Carnelian?'

'What *is* an imposture?'

She looked up in surprise and then she laughed. 'Oh, dear, Mr Carnelian! Oh dear! What are we to do?'

He took her hand and she did not resist him. He began to lead her up the bank. We'll go to the people who live in the laboratories I've just spotted. They'll help us.'

'Laboratories. How do you know?'

'Robot workers. You don't have many in 1896, do you?'

'We have none at all, as far as I've heard!'

'Then I am right. It is of an experimental nature. We shall find scientists there. And scientists will not only understand what I have to say – they'll be more than glad to be of assistance!'

'I am not at all sure, Mr Carnelian – Oh!' She had reached the fence, she was looking at the scene below them. First she blushed and then she laughed. 'Oh, Mr Carnelian, I'm afraid your hopes are unjustified. I wondered what the smell might be ...'

'Smell? Is it unusual?'

'A little. Oh, my goodness...'

'It is not an experimental farm, Mrs Underwood?' For the first time his spirits threatened to desert him.

'No, Mr Carnelian. It is what we call a sewage farm.' She leaned on the fence and as she laughed tears ran down her cheeks.

'What is "sewage"?' he asked.

'It is not something a lady could tell you, I fear!'

He sat down on the ground at her feet. He put his head in his hands and he became aware of a hint of despair in the back of his mind.

'Then how are we to find a time machine?' he said. 'Even an old one, even that broken one I left behind on my last visit – it would be *something*. Ah, Mrs Underwood, I think I have not planned this adventure as well as I might have done.'

'Perhaps that is why I am beginning to enjoy it,' she said. 'Cheer up, Mr Carnelian. My father always used to tell me that there was nothing like a good, solid, seemingly unsolvable problem to get one's teeth into and take one's mind off the usual silly anxieties which plague us. And this problem is huge – it certainly makes any others I might have had seem very trivial indeed! I must admit I had sunk into self-pity and that will never do. But I am over that now.'

'I suspect that I am only just beginning to discover what it is,' said Jherek feelingly. 'Does it involve a belief in an anthropomorphical and malevolent being called Fate?'

'I'm afraid it does, Mr Carnelian.'

He pulled himself slowly to his feet. She helped him on with his coat. He brightened at the next thought which occurred to him. 'Perhaps, however, it is furthering my "moral education"? Would that be the case, Mrs Underwood?'

They began to climb down the bank and back to the sandy path.

This time she took him by the hand. 'It's more in the nature of a side-effect, though I know I shouldn't sound so cynical. Mr Underwood has often said to me that there is nothing so unwelcome in the sight of the Lord than a cynical woman. And there are a great many of them about, I'm afraid, in these worldly and upsetting modern times of ours. Come along, let's see where this path takes us.'

'I hope,' he murmured, 'that it is not back to Bromley.'

CHAPTER FIFTEEN

ENTRAINED FOR THE METROPOLIS

The small sandy-haired man unscrewed the ebony and glass object from his right eye and sucked somewhat noisily at his teeth. 'Funny,' he said. 'It's a cut above yer usual paste. I'll give ya that much. But it's no more a real ruby than the kind ya kin by fer a shillin' in the market. Settin's nice, though, I can't recognize the metal. Well, 'ow much d'yer wanna borrow on it?' He held out Jherek's power ring on the palm of his hand.

Mrs Underwood stood nervously beside Jherek at the counter. 'A sovereign?'

'I dunno.' He looked at it again. 'It's a curiosity, an' beautiful workmanship, I'll grant ... But what do I risk?

Fifteen bob?'

'Very well,' said Mrs Underwood. She accepted the money on Jherek's behalf. He was half-stupefied by the negotiations, having no clear idea of what was taking place. He didn't mind losing a power ring, for he could easily get another on his return and they were useless here, but he could not quite understand why Mrs Underwood was giving it to this man and why the man was giving her something in exchange. She accepted a ticket and tucked it into his top pocket.

They left the shop and entered a busy street. 'Luckily it's market day and we shan't be too noticeable,' said Mrs Underwood. 'Gypsies and so on will be about, as well.' Carts and carriages jammed the narrow roadway and a couple of motorcars added to the confusion, their fumes giving rise to a great deal of pointed coughing and loud complaints from those on foot. 'We'll have something to eat at the station buffet, while we are waiting for the train. Once in London, we'll go straight to the Café Royale and hope that one of your friends is there. It is our only chance.' She walked as rapidly as possible up the winding pavement of the country street, turning into an alley blocked by two posts; the alley became a series of stone steps. They climbed them and found themselves in a much quieter road. 'The station's this way, I believe,' she said. 'It is a stroke of luck that we were so close to Orpington.'

They approached a green and red building. It was indeed, the railway station and Mrs Underwood marched boldly to the ticket office and bought them two Second Class single tickets to Charing Cross. 'We have twenty minutes to wait,' she said, glancing at the clock over the ticket office, 'ample time for refreshments. And,' she added in an undertone, 'there are no police in evidence. We appear for the moment to have made good our escape.'

It was Jherek's first encounter with the cheese sandwich.

He found it rather hard going, but he made the most of the experience, telling himself that, after all, he might not have the chance again. He enjoyed the tea, finding it rather nicer than the beverage he had had at Mrs Underwood's, and when, at last, the train came steaming into the station he cried out in delight: 'It is just like my own little engine at home!'

Mrs Underwood seemed embarrassed. Some of the other people in the refreshment room were looking at Jherek and whispering among themselves. But Jherek hardly noticed. He was dragging Mrs Underwood eagerly through the doors and onto the platform.

'Orping*ton*,' called a thin man in a dark uniform. '*Or*pington!'

Jherek waited impatiently for some passengers to leave their carriage and he climbed in, nodding and smiling to those who were already seated.

'Isn't it splendid?' he said to her as they sat down. 'Ancient transport has always been one of my chief enthusiasms – as you know.'

'Please try to say as little as possible,' she begged him in a whisper. She had already warned him that the newspapers would have published reports of their adventures of the previous night. He apologized and settled back, but he could not resist peering animatedly out of the windows at the scenery as it went past.

Mrs Underwood seemed particularly distraught by the time they reached Charing Cross. Before leaving the carriage, she leaned out of the open window and then waited until all the other passengers had gone before saying to Jherek: 'I cannot see any sign that the police are waiting for us. But we must hurry.'

They joined the crowds making their way towards the barriers at the far end of the platforms and here even Jherek was conscious that they did not quite look the same as the others. Mrs Underwood's dress was muddy, crumpled and torn in a couple of places; also she wore no hat, whereas all the other ladies had hats, veils, sunshades and coats. Jherek's black coat was stained and as battered as Mrs Underwood's dress and he had a large hole in the knee of his left trouser leg. As they reached the gate and handed their tickets to the collector, they attracted some comment as well as disapproving glances. And it was Jherek who saw the policeman come walking ponderously towards them, his tongue thoughtfully stroking his lower lip, his hands clasped behind his back.

'Run, Mrs Underwood!' he shouted urgently.

And then it was too late for her to brazen out the confrontation for the policeman was saying: 'By Golly, it is them!' and was beginning to pull a whistle from his pocket.

They dashed for the exit, blundering first into a very large woman carrying a basket and leading a very small black and white dog on a piece of string, who cried ''ere, watch it!' rather too late; then into two maiden ladies who cackled like startled hens and said a great deal concerning the manners of the young; and lastly into a stout stockbroker in a hat of exaggerated height and sleekness, who grunted 'Bless my soul!' and sat down on a fruitstall so that the fruitstall collapsed and sent apples, grapefruit, oranges and pineapples rolling about in all directions, causing the policeman to interrupt his attempts to blow his whistle as he dodged a veritable Niagara of pears, calling after them: 'Stop there! Stop, I say, in the name of the Law!'

Outside the station they found themselves in the Strand and now Jherek saw something leaning against a wall on the corner of Villiers Street.

'Look!, Mrs Underwood – we are saved. A time machine!'

'That, Mr Carnelian, is a tandem bicycle.'

He already had his hands on it and was trying to straddle it as he had seen the others do.

'We would do better to hail a cab,' she said.

'Get aboard quickly. Can you see any controls?'

With a sigh, she took the remaining saddle, in the

front. 'We had best head for Regent Street. It is not far, happily. The other side of Piccadilly. At least this will prove to you, once and for all, that ...'

Her voice was lost as they hurtled into the press of the traffic, weaving between trams and omnibuses, between horses and motor cars and causing both to come to sudden stops and stand stock still in the middle of the road, panting and shuddering.

Jherek, expecting to see the scene vanish at any moment, paid little attention to the confusion happening around them. He was having a great deal of trouble keeping his balance upon the time machine.

'It will be soon!' he cried into her ear, 'it *must* be soon!' And he pedalled harder. All that happened was that the machine lurched onto the pavement, shot across Trafalgar Square at considerable speed, up the Haymarket, and was in Leicester Square almost before they had realized it. Here Jherek fell off the tandem, to the vast entertainment of a crowd of street urchins hanging about outside the doors of the Empire Theatre of Varieties.

'It doesn't seem to work,' he said.

Mrs Underwood informed him that she had told him so. She now had a large tear in the hem of her dress where it had caught in the chain. However, for the moment, they did not appear to have the police on their trail.

'Quickly,' she said, 'and let us pray to heaven that someone who knows you is in the Café Royale!'

Heads turned as they ran across Piccadilly Circus and arrived at last at the doors of the Café Royale which Jherek had last visited less than twenty-four hours before. Mrs Underwood pushed at the doors, but they would not budge. 'Oh goodness!' she said in despair. 'It's closed!'

'Closed?' said Jherek. He pressed his face to the glass. He could see people inside. He signed to them, but they shook their hands from side to side and pointed at the clock.

'Closed,' sighed Mrs Underwood. She uttered a funny, toneless laugh. 'Well, that's it! We're finished!'

'Hey!' called someone. They turned, ready to run, but it was not the police. From the great tide of traffic converging upon Piccadilly Circus they distinguished a hansom cab, its driver seated high in the rear of the vehicle, his face expressionless. 'Hi!' said a voice from within the cab.

'Mr Harris!' called Jherek, recognizing the face. 'We were hoping you would be in the Café Royale.'

'Get in!' hissed Harris. 'Hurry. Both of you.'

Mrs Underwood lost no time in accepting his offer and soon the three of them were crammed in the cab and it was jogging around the Circus and back towards Leicester Square.

'You *are* the young man I saw yesterday,' said Harris in triumph. 'I thought so. This is a bit of luck.'

'Luck for us, Mr Harris,' said Mrs Underwood, 'but not for you if your part in this is discovered.'

'Oh, I've bluffed my way out of worse situations,' he said. He laughed easily. 'Besides, I'm a journalist first and foremost – and we newshounds are permitted a certain amount of leeway when obtaining a really tip-top story. I'm not just helping you out of altruism, you know. I read the papers today. They're saying that you're the Mayfair Killer come back from the dead to be re-united with your – um – paramour!' Mr Harris's eyes gleamed. 'What's your version? You certainly bear a striking resemblance to the Killer. I saw a drawing in one of the papers when the trial was taking place. And you, young lady, were a witness for the defence at the trial, were you not?'

She looked at Mr Harris a little suspiciously. It seemed to Jherek that she did not altogether like the bluff, rapid-speaking editor of the *Saturday Review*.

He saw that she hesitated and raised his hand. 'Say no more at this stage! What reason, after all, have you to trust me.' With his stick he opened a hatch at the top of the cab. 'I have changed my mind, cabby. Take us, instead, to Bloomsbury Square.' He let the flap fall back and turning to them said, 'I have rooms there where you will be safe for the moment.'

'Why are you helping us, Mr Harris?'

'I want an exclusive of your story, ma'am, for one thing. Also, there were facts about the Mayfair case which never seemed to fit right. I am curious to know what you can tell me.'

'You could help us with the Law?' Hope now overcame her caution.

'I have many friends,' said Mr Harris, stroking his chin with the head of his cane, 'in the Law. I am on intimate terms with several High Court Judges, Queen's Counsels – eminent lawyers of all descriptions. I think you could call me a man of influence, ma'am.'

'Then we may yet be saved,' said Mrs Underwood.

CHAPTER SIXTEEN

THE MYSTERIOUS MR JACKSON

After installing Mrs Underwood and Jherek Carnelian in his Bloomsbury rooms, Mr Harris left, telling them that he would return as soon as possible and that they were to make themselves comfortable. The rooms, it seemed, did not really meet with Mrs Underwood's approval, though Jherek found them extremely pleasant. There were numerous pictures of attractive young people upon the walls, there were thick velvet curtains at the windows, and deep-piled Turkish carpets upon the floors. There were porcelain figurines and a profusion of jade and amber ornaments. Looking through the books, Jherek found a great many elegant drawings of a kind he had not previously seen and he showed them to Mrs Underwood, hoping that they might cheer her up, but instead she closed the books with a bang, refusing to explain why she would not look at the pictures. He was disappointed, for he had hoped that she would help the time pass by reading to him from the books. He found some other books, with yellow paper covers, which did not have pictures, and handed one of these to her.

'Perhaps you could read this?'

She glanced at it and sniffed. 'It is *French*,' she said.

'You do not like it, either?'

'It is French.' She looked through into the bedroom, at the wide bed with its lavish coverings. 'This whole place reeks of the *fin de siècle*. Although Mr Harris has helped us, I do not have to approve of his morals. I am in no doubt as to his purposes in keeping these rooms.'

'Purposes? Does he not live in them?'

'Live? Oh, yes. To the full, it seems. But I suspect this is not the address at which he entertains his respectable friends.' She crossed to a window and flung it up. 'If he has any,' she added. 'I wonder how long we shall have to stay here.'

'Until Mr Harris has time to talk to a few people he knows and to take down our story,' said Jherek, repeating what Mr Harris had told them. 'There is a great sense of safety about this apartment, Mrs Underwood. Don't you feel it?'

'It has been designed to avoid ordinary public scrutiny,' she said, and she sniffed again. Then she stared into one of the long gilt mirrors and tried, as she had tried before, to tidy her hair.

'Aren't you tired?' Jherek walked into the bedroom. 'We could lie down. We could sleep.'

'So we could,' she said sharply. 'I suspect that there is more lying down than standing up goes on here, as a rule. Art nouveau everywhere! Purple plumes and incense. This is where Mr Harris entertains his actresses.'

'Oh,' said Jherek, having given up trying to understand

her. He accepted, however, that there was something wrong with the rooms. He wished that Mrs Underwood had been able to complete his moral education; if she had, he felt, he, too, might be able to enjoy sniffing and pursing his lips, for there was not much doubt that she *was* taking a certain pleasure in her activities: her cheeks were quite flushed, there was a light in her eyes. 'Actresses?'

'So-called.'

'There does not seem much in the way of food here,' he told her, 'but there are lots of bottles. Would you like something to drink?'

'No thank you, Mr Carnelian. Unless there is some mineral water.'

'You had better look for yourself, Mrs Underwood. I don't know which is which.'

Hesitantly, she entered the bedroom and surveyed the wide selection on a small sideboard set against the wall. 'Mr Harris appears to have a distaste for Adam's Ale,' she said. Her head lifted as there came a knocking upon the outer door. 'Who could that be?'

'Mr Harris returning earlier than expected?'

'Possibly. Open the door, Mr Carnelian, but have a care. I do not entirely trust your journalist friend.'

Jherek had some difficulty with the catch and the light knocking sounded again before he had the door open. When he saw who stood there, he grinned with relief and pleasure. 'Oh, Jagged, dear Jagged! At last! It is you!'

The handsome man in the doorway removed his hat. 'The name,' he said, 'is Jackson. I believe I saw you briefly last night at the Café Royale? You would be Mr Carnelian.'

'Come in, devious Jagged!'

With a slight bow to Mrs Underwood, who stood now in the centre of the sitting room, Lord Jagged of Canaria entered. 'You would be Mrs Underwood? My name is Jackson. I work for the *Saturday Review*. Mr Harris sent me to take some shorthand notes. He will join us later.'

'You are the judge!' she exclaimed. 'You are Lord Jagger, who sentenced Mr Carnelian to death!'

The man who claimed to be Mr Jackson raised his eyebrows as, with a delicate movement, he divested himself of his top-coat and laid it, together with his hat, gloves and stick, upon the table. 'Mr Harris warned me that you would still be a little agitated. It is understandable, madam, in the circumstances. I assure you that I am neither of the two men so far mentioned. I am merely Jackson – a journalist. My job is to put some basic questions to you. Mr Harris sent his regards and said that he is doing everything in his power to contact someone in high places – who must for the moment be nameless – in the hope that they will be able to assist you.'

'You bear a remarkable resemblance to the Lord Chief Justice,' she said.

'So I have been told. But I am neither as eminent nor as talented as that gentleman, to my regret.'

Jherek was laughing. 'Listen to him! Isn't he perfect!'

'Mr Carnelian,' she said, 'I think you are making a mistake. You will embarrass Mr Jackson.'

'No, no!' Mr Jackson dismissed the suggestion with a wave of his slender hand. 'We journalists are pretty hardy fellows, you know.'

Jherek shrugged. 'If you are not Jagged – and Jagged was not Jagger – then I must assume there are a number of Jaggeds, each playing different rôles, perhaps throughout history...'

Mr Jackson smiled and produced a notebook and a pencil. 'That's the stuff,' he said. 'We seem to have a rival to your friend Mr Wells, eh, Mrs Underwood?'

'Mr Wells is not my friend,' she said.

'You know him, however, don't you – Mr Jackson?' asked Jherek.

'Only slightly. We've had the odd conversation in the past. I've read a good many of his books, however. If your story is up to *The Wonderful Visit* and can be presented in the right way, then our circulation's assured!' He settled himself comfortably in a deep armchair. Jherek and Mrs Underwood sat on the edge of the ottoman opposite him. 'Now, I gather you're claiming to be the Mayfair Killer returned from the dead...'

'Not at all!' exclaimed Mrs Underwood. 'Mr Carnelian would not kill anyone.'

'Unfairly accused, then? Returned to vindicate the claim? Oh, this is splendid stuff!'

'I haven't *been* dead,' said Jherek. 'Not recently at any rate. And I don't understand about the rest.'

'You are on the wrong tack, I fear, Mr Jackson,' said Mrs Underwood primly.

'Where *have* you been, then, Mr Carnelian?'

'In my own time – in Jagged's time – in the distant future, of course. I am a time traveller, just as Mrs Underwood is.' He touched her hand, but she removed it quickly. 'That is how we met.'

'You honestly believe that you have travelled through time, Mr Carnclian?'

'Of course. Oh, Jagged, is there any point to this? You've already played this game once before!'

Mr Jackson turned his attention to Mrs Underwood. 'And you say that you visited the future? That you met Mr Carnelian there? You fell in love?'

'Mr Carnelian was kind to me. He rescued me from imprisonment.'

'Aha! And you were able to do the same for him here?'

'No. I am still not sure *how* he escaped death on the gallows, but escape he did – went back to his own time – then returned. Was it only last night? To Bromley.'

'Your husband then called the police.'

'Inadvertently, the police must have been called, yes. My husband was over-excited. Have you heard how he is, by the way?'

'I have only read the papers. He is quoted, in the more sensational sheets, as claiming that you have been leading a double-life – by day a respectable, God-fearing Bromley housewife – by night, an accomplice of thieves – "A

Female Charlie Peace" I believe you were termed in today's *Police Gazette*.'

'Oh, no! Then my reputation is gone for good.'

Mr Jackson inspected the cuff of his shirt. 'It would seem that it would take much, Mrs Underwood, to restore it. You know how the odour of scandal clings, long after the scandal itself is proved unfounded.'

She straightened her shoulders. 'It remains my duty to try to convince Harold that I am not the wanton creature he now believes me to be. It will cause him much grief if he thinks that I have been deceiving him over a period of time. I can still attempt to put his mind at rest on that issue.'

'Doubtless ...' murmured Mr Jackson, and his pencil moved rapidly across the page of his notebook. 'Now, could we have a description of the future?' He returned his attention to Jherek. 'An Anarchist Utopia, is it, perhaps? You are an anarchist, are you not, sir?'

'I don't know what one is,' said Jherek.

'He certainly is not!' cried Mrs Underwood. 'A degree of anarchy might have *resulted* from his actions ...'

'A Socialist Utopia, then?'

'I think I follow your meaning now, Mr Jackson,' said Mrs Underwood. 'You believe Mr Carnelian to be some kind of mad political assassin, claiming to be from an ideal future in the hope of propagating his message?'

'Well, I wondered ...'

'Was this idea original to you?'

'Mr Harris suggested —'

'I suspected as much. He did not believe a word of our story!'

'He considered it a trifle over-coloured, Mrs Underwood. Would you not think so, if you heard it, say, from *my* lips!'

'I wouldn't!' smiled Jherek. 'Because I know who you are.'

'Do be quiet, please, Mr Carnelian,' said Mrs Underwood. 'You are in danger of confusing matters again.'

'You are beginning to confuse *me,* I fear,' said Mr Jackson equably.

'Then we are only reciprocating, joking Jagged, the confusion you have created in us!' Jherek Carnelian got up and strode across the room. 'You know that the Morphail Effect is supposed to apply in all cases of time travel to the past, whether by travellers who are returning to their own time, or those merely visiting the past from some future age.'

'I'm afraid that I have not heard of this "Morphail Effect"? Some new theory?'

Ignoring him, Jherek continued. 'I now suspect that the Morphail Effect only applies in the case of those who produce a sufficient number of paradoxes to "register" as it were upon the fabric of Time. Those who are careful to disguise their origins, to do little to make use of any information they might have of the future, are allowed to exist in the past for as long as they wish!'

'I'm not sure I entirely follow you, Mr Carnelian. However, please go on.' Mr Jackson continued to take notes.

'If you publish all this, Mr Carnelian will be judged thoroughly mad,' said Mrs Underwood quietly.

'If you tell enough people what I have told you – it will send us off into the future again, probably.' Jherek offered Mr Jackson an intelligent stare. 'Wouldn't it, Jagged?'

Mr Jackson said apologetically. 'I'm still not quite with you. However, just keep talking and I'll keep taking notes.'

'I don't think I'll say anything for a while,' said Jherek. 'I must think this over.'

'Mr Jackson *could* help us, if he would accept the truth,' said Mrs Underwood. 'But if he is of the same opinion as Mr Harris...'

'I am a reporter,' said Mr Jackson. 'I keep my theories to myself, Mrs Underwood. All I wish to do is my job. If you had some proof, for instance...'

'Show him that odd-looking gun you have, Mr Carnelian.'

Jherek felt in the pocket of his coat and pulled the deceptor-gun out. 'It's hardly proof,' he said.

'It is certainly a very bizarre design,' said Mr Jackson, inspecting it.

He was holding it in his hands when there came a knocking on the door and a voice bellowed:

'Open this door! Open in the name of the Law!'

'The police!' Mrs Underwood's hand went to her mouth. 'Mr Harris has betrayed us!'

The door shook as heavy bodies flung themselves against it.

Mr Jackson got up slowly, handing back the gun to Jherek. 'I think we had better let them in,' he said.

'You knew they were coming!' cried Mrs Underwood accusingly. 'Oh, we have been deceived on all sides.'

'I doubt if Mr Harris knew. On the other hand, you were brought here in an ordinary cab. The police could have discovered the address from the cabby. It's rather typical of Frank Harris to forget, as it were, those all-important details.'

Mr Jackson called out: 'Wait one moment, please. We are about to unlock the door!' He smiled encouragingly at Mrs Underwood as he undid the catch and flung the door wide. 'Good afternoon, inspector.'

A man in a heavy ulster, with a small bowler hat fixed rigidly upon the top of his rocklike head, walked with massive bovine dignity into the room. He looked about him, he sniffed rather as Mrs Underwood had sniffed; pointedly, he looked neither at Jherek Carnelian nor at Mrs Underwood. Then he said:

'Herr-um!'

He wheeled, a cunning rhino, his finger jutting forward like a menacing horn, until it was quite close to Jherek's nose. 'You 'im?'

'Who?'

'Mayfair Killer?'

'No.' Jherek inched backwards.

'Thought not.' He fingered a thoroughly well-waxed moustache. 'I'm Inspector Springer.' He brought bushy brows down over deep, brooding eyes. 'Of Scotland Yard,' he said. '*Heard* of me, 'ave you?'

'I'm afraid not,' said Jherek.

'I deal with politicals, with aliens, with disruptive forrin' elements – an' I deal with 'em extremely *firm.*'

'So you believe it, too!' Mrs Underwood rose. 'You are mistaken in your suspicions, inspector.'

'We'll see,' said Inspector Springer cryptically. He raised a finger and cocked it, ordering four or five uniformed men into the room. 'I *know* my anarchists, lady. All three of yer have that particular look abart yer. We're goin' to do some very thorough checkin' indeed. *Very* thorough.'

'You're on the wrong track, I think,' said Mr Jackson. 'I'm a journalist. I was interviewing these people and ...'

'So you say, sir. Wrong track, eh? Well, we'll soon get on the right one, never fear.' He looked at the deceptor-gun and stretched out his hand to receive it. 'Give me that there weapon,' he said. 'It don't look *English* ter *me.*'

'I think you'd better fire it, Jherek,' said Mr Jackson softly. 'There doesn't seem to be a lot of choice.'

'Fire it, Jagged?'

Mr Jackson shrugged. 'I think so.'

Jherek pulled the trigger. 'There's only about one charge left in it ...'

The room in Bloomsbury Square was suddenly occupied by fifteen warriors of the late Cannibal Empire period. Their triangular faces were painted green, their bodies blue, and they were naked save for bangles and necklaces of small skulls and finger-bones. In their hands were long spears with barbed, rusted points, and spiked clubs. They were female. As they grinned, they revealed yellow, filed teeth.

'I *knew* you was ruddy anarchists!' said Inspector Springer triumphantly.

His men had fallen back to the door, but Inspector Springer held his ground. 'Arrest them!' he ordered severely.

The green and blue lady warriors gibbered and seemed to advance upon him. They licked calloused lips.

'This way,' whispered Mr Jackson, leading Jherek and Mrs Underwood into the bedroom. He opened a window and climbed out onto a small balcony. They joined him as he balanced for a moment on one balustrade and then jumped gracefully to the next. A flight of steps had been built up to this adjoining balcony and it was an easy matter to descend by means of the steps to the ground. Mr Jackson strolled through a small yard and opened a gate in a wall which led into a secluded, leafy street.

'Jagged – it *must* be you. You knew what the deceptor-gun would do!'

'My dear fellow,' said Mr Jackson coolly, 'I merely realized that you possessed a weapon and that it could be useful to us in our predicament.'

'Where do we go now?' Mrs Underwood asked in a small, pathetic voice.

'Oh, Jagged will help us get back to the future,' Jherek told her confidently. 'Won't you, Jagged?'

Mr Jackson seemed faintly amused. 'Even if I were this friend of yours, there would be no reason to assume, surely, that I can skip back and forth through time at will, any more than can you!'

'I had not considered that,' said Jherek. 'You are merely an experimenter, then? An experimenter little further advanced in your investigations than am I?'

Mr Jackson said nothing.

'And are we part of that experiment, Lord Jagged?' Jherek continued. 'Are my experiences proving of help to you?'

Mr Jackson shrugged. 'I could enjoy our conversations better,' he said, 'if we were in a more secure position.

Now we are, all three, "on the run". I suggest we repair to my rooms in Soho and there review our situation. I will contact Mr Harris and get fresh instructions. This, of course, will prove embarrassing for him, too!' He led the way through the back streets. It was evening and the sun was beginning to set.

Mrs Underwood fell back a step or two, tugging at Jherek's sleeve. 'I believe that we are being duped,' she whispered. 'For some reason, we are being used to further the ends of either Mr Harris or Mr Jackson or both. We might stand a better chance on our own, since obviously the police do not believe, any longer, that you are an escaped murderer.'

'They believe me an anarchist, instead. Isn't that worse?'

'Luckily, not in the eyes of the Law.'

'Then where can we go?'

'Do you know where this Mr Wells lives?'

'Yes, the Café Royale. I saw him there.'

'Then we must try to get back to the Café Royale. He does not *live* there, exactly, Mr Carnelian – but we can hope that he spends a great deal of his time there.'

'You must explain the difference to me,' he said.

Ahead of them Mr Jackson was hailing a cab, but when he turned to tell them to get in, they were already in another street and running as fast as their weary legs would carry them.

CHAPTER SEVENTEEN

A PARTICULARLY MEMORABLE NIGHT AT THE CAFÉ ROYALE

It was dark by the time Mrs Underwood had managed to find her way to the Café Royale. They had kept to the back streets after she had, in a second-hand clothing shop near the British Museum, purchased a large, tattered shawl for herself and a moth-eaten raglan to cover Jherek's ruined suit. Now, she had assured him, they looked like any other couple belonging to the London poor. It was true that they no longer attracted any attention. It was not until they tried to go through the doors of the Café Royale that they found themselves once again in difficulties. As they entered a waiter came rushing up. He spoke in a quiet, urgent and commanding voice.

'Shove off, the pair of yer! My word, I never thought I'd see the day beggars got so bloomin' bold!'

There were not many customers in the restaurant, but those who were there had begun to comment.

'Shove off, will yer!' said the waiter in a louder voice. 'I'll git the peelers on yer...' He had gone quite red in the face.

Jherek Carnelian ignored him, for he had seen Frank Harris sitting at a small table in the company of a lady of exotic appearance. She wore a bright carmine dress, trimmed with black lace, a black mantilla, and had several silver combs in her raven hair. She was laughing in a rather high-pitched, artificial way at something Mr Harris had just said.

'Mr Harris!' called Jherek Carnelian.

'Mr *Harris*!' Mrs Underwood said fiercely. Undaunted by the agitated waiters, she began to stalk towards the table. 'I should appreciate a word with you, sir!'

'Oh, my God!' Mr Harris groaned. 'I thought you were still ... How? Oh, my God!'

The lady in carmine turned to see what was happening. Her lips matched her dress. In a rather frigid tone she said: 'This lady is a friend of yours, Mr Harris?'

He clutched for his companion's hand. 'Donna Isobella, I assure you – two people I gave my protection to – um...'

'Your *protection*, Mr Harris, seems worth very little.' Mrs Underwood looked Donna Isobella up and down. 'Is this, then, the highly placed person with whom I understood you to be in conference?'

There came a chorus of complaints from other tables. The waiter seized Jherek Carnelian by the arm. Jherek, mildly surprised, stared down at him. 'Yes?'

'You *must* leave, sir. I can see now that you are a gentleman – but you are improperly dressed...'

'It is all I have,' said Jherek. 'My power rings, you see, are useless here.'

'I don't understand...'

Kindly, Jherek showed the waiter his remaining rings. 'They all have slightly different functions. This one is chiefly used for biological restructuring. This one...'

'Oh, my God!' said Mr Harris again.

A new voice interrupted. It was excited and loud. 'There they are! I told you we should find them in this sinkhole of iniquity!'

Mr Underwood did not appear to have slept for some time. He still wore the suit Jherek had seen him in the previous night. His hay-coloured hair was still in disarray. His pince-nez clung lopsidedly to his nose.

Behind Mr Underwood stood Inspector Springer and his men. They looked a little dazed.

Several customers got up and called for their hats and coats. Only Mr Harris and Donna Isobella remained seated. Mr Harris had his head in his hands. Donna Isobella was staring brightly around her smiling at everyone now. Silver flashed; carmine rustled. She seemed pleased by the interruption.

'Seize them!' demanded Mr Underwood.

'Harold,' began Mrs Underwood, 'there has been a terrible mistake! I am not the woman you believe me to be!'

'To be sure, madam! To be sure!'

'I mean that I am innocent of the sins with which you charge me, my dear!'

'Ha!'

Inspector Springer and his men began to weave their way somewhat warily towards the small group on the far side of the restaurant, while Harold Underwood brought up the rear.

Mr Harris was trying to recover his position with Donna Isobella. 'My connection with these people is only of the most slender, Donna Isobella.'

'No matter how slender, I wish to meet them,' she said. 'Introduce us, please, Frank!'

It was when the Lat brigand-musicians materialized that many of the waiters left with the few customers who had remained.

Captain Mubbers, his instrument at the ready, stared distractedly around him. The pupils of his single eye began slowly to focus. 'Ferkit!' he growled belligerently, at no one in particular. 'Kroofrudi!'

Inspector Springer paused in his stride and stared thoughtfully down at the seven small aliens. With the air of a man who is on the brink of discovering a profound truth, he murmured: 'Ho!'

'Smakfrub, glex mibix cue?' said one of Captain Mubbers' crew-members. And with his instrument he feinted at Inspector Springer's legs. Evidently they had the same problem, in that their weapons could not work at this distance from their power source, or else the charges had run out.

The Lat's three pupils crossed alarmingly and then fled apart. He mumbled to himself, turning his back on Inspector Springer. His ears shrugged.

'The rest of your anarchist gang, eh?' said Inspector Springer. 'And even more desperate-looking than the last lot. What's the lingo? Some kind a' Roossian, is it?'

'They are the Lat,' said Jherek. 'They must have got caught in the field Nurse set up. Now we *do* have a paradox. They're space-travellers,' he explained to Mrs Underwood, 'from my own time...'

'Any of you speak English?' enquired Inspector Springer of Captain Mubbers.

'Hawtyard!' Captain Mubbers growled.

''Ere, I say, steady on!' expostulated Inspector Springer. 'Ladies,' he said, 'at least of sorts, are in the company.'

One of his men, indicating the striped flannel suits which each of the Lat wore, suggested that they might have escaped from prison – for all that the suits resembled pyjamas.

'Those are not their normal clothes,' said Jherek. 'Nurse put them into those when...'

'Nobody *arsked* you, sir, if you don't mind,' said Inspector Springer haughtily. 'We'll take your statement in a moment.'

'Those are the ones you must arrest, officer!' insisted Harold Underwood, still shaking with rage. He indicated his wife and Jherek.

'It's astonishing,' said Mrs Underwood half to herself, 'how you can live with someone for such a long time without realizing the heights of passion to which they are capable of rising.'

Inspector Springer reached towards Captain Mubbers. The Lat's bulbous nose seemed to pulse with rage. Captain Mubbers looked up at Inspector Springer and glared. The policeman tried to lay his hand on Captain Mubbers' shoulder. Then he withdrew the hand sharply.

'Eouw!' he exclaimed, nursing the injured limb. 'Little beggar bit me!' He turned in desperation to Jherek. 'Can you talk their lingo?'

'I'm afraid not,' said Jherek. 'Translation pills are only good for one language at a time and currently I am talking and hearing yours...'

Inspector Springer appeared to dismiss Jherek from his mind for the moment. 'The others just vanished,' he said, aggrievedly, convinced that someone had deliberately deceived him.

'*They* were illusions,' Jherek told him. '*These* are real – space-travellers...'

Again Inspector Springer made a movement towards Captain Mubbers. 'Jillip goff!' Captain Mubbers demanded. And he kicked Inspector Springer sharply in the shins with one of his hoof-like feet.

'Eouw!' said Inspector Springer again. 'All right! Yer arsked fer it!' And his expression became ugly.

Captain Mubbers pushed aside a table. Silver-ware clattered to the floor. Two of his crew, their attention drawn to the knives and forks, fell upon their knees and began to gather the implements up, chattering excitedly as if they had just discovered buried treasure.

'Leave that cutlery alone!' bellowed Inspector Springer.

'All right, men! Charge 'em!'

To a man, the constables produced their truncheons, and were upon the Lat, who fought back with the tableware as well as their powerless instrument-weapons.

Mr Jackson came strolling in. There were now no waiters to be seen. He hung up his own hat and coat, taking only a mild interest in the mêlée at the centre of the restaurant, and crossed to where Frank Harris sat moaning softly to himself, Donna Isobella sat clapping her hands and giggling, and Jherek Carnelian and Mrs Underwood stood wondering what to do. Harold Underwood was waving his fists, leaping around the periphery of the fight shouting at Inspector Springer to do his duty (he did not seem to believe that the inspector's duty had much to do with arresting three-foot high brigand-musicians from a distant galaxy).

'Good evening to you,' said Mr Jackson affably. He opened a slender gold case and extracted an Egyptian cigarette. Inserting it into a holder, he lit it with a match and, leaning against a pillar, proceeded to watch the fight. 'I thought I'd find you here,' he added.

Jherek was quite enjoying himself. 'And I might have guessed that you would come, Jagged. Who would want to miss this?'

It seemed that none of his friends wished to do so, for now, their costumes blazing and putting to shame the opulence of the Café Royale, the Iron Orchid, the Duke of Queens, Bishop Castle and My Lady Charlotina appeared.

The Iron Orchid, in particular, was delighted to see her son, but when she spoke he discovered that he could not understand her. Feeling in his pockets, he produced the rest of his translation pills and handed them to the four newcomers. They were quick to realize the situation and each swallowed a pill.

'I thought at first it was another illusion from your deceptor-gun,' the Iron Orchid told him, 'but actually we are back in the Dawn Age, are we not, with you?'

'You are, indeed, tenderest of blooms. You see, I am re-united with Mrs Underwood.'

'Good evening,' said Mrs Underwood to Jherek's mother in a tone which might have contained a hint of coolness.

'Good evening, my dear. Your costume is beautiful. It is contemporary, I suppose?' The Iron Orchid turned in a swirl of fiery drapery. 'And Jagged is here, too! Greetings to you, languid Lord of Canaria!'

Mr Jackson smiled faintly in acknowledgement.

Bishop Castle gathered his blue gown about him and sat down next to Mr Harris and Donna Isobella. 'I am glad to be out of that wood, at any rate,' he said. 'Are you residents of this age, or visitors like myself?'

Donna Isobella beamed at him. 'I am from Spain,' she said. 'I dance. Exotically, you know.'

'How delightful. Are the Lat causing you much trouble?'

'The little beast-men? Oh, no. They and the police are entertaining themselves quite cheerfully, I think.'

With a shaking hand, Mr Harris poured himself a large glass of champagne. He did not offer any to the others. He drank rapidly.

My Lady Charlotina kissed Mrs Underwood upon the cheek. 'Oh, you can scarcely know the excitement you have caused us all, pretty ancestress. But your own age seems not without its diversions!' She went to join Bishop Castle at the table.

The Duke of Queens was exclaiming with great pleasure about the plush and gilt decor of the restaurant. 'I am determined to make one,' he announced. 'What did you say it was called, Jherek?'

'The Café Royale.'

'It shall flourish again, five times the size, at the End of Time!' proclaimed the Duke.

From the middle of the room came muffled cries of 'Ferkit!' and 'Eouw!' Neither Inspector Springer's team, nor Captain Mubbers', seemed to be getting the upper hand. More tables were turned over.

The Duke of Queens took careful note of the police uniforms. 'Does this happen every evening? Presumably the Lat are a new addition to the programme?'

'I think the best they've done in the past are drunken revels of the conventional sort,' said Mr Jackson. 'Though they are not so very different in essence, I suppose.'

'The Café is well known,' Donna Isobella was explaining to an intensely interested Bishop Castle, 'for its Bohemian clientele. It is rather less formal than most restaurants of its class.'

There came a queer whizzing noise now and a flash of light which blinded them all, then Brannart Morphail was hanging near the ceiling in a harness of pulsing yellow, with what appeared to be two rapidly spinning discs upon his back, threatening to collide with a large crystal chandelier. His medical boot waved back and forth in an agitated way as he slapped at part of the harness near his shoulder, evidently finding difficulty in controlling the machine.

'I warned you! I warned you!' he cried from on high. His voice was crackling, improperly modulated, as if he were using an inferior translator. It rose and fell. 'All this manipulation of time is creating havoc! No good will come of it! Beware! Beware!'

Even the police and the Lat paused in their battle to stare up at the apparition.

Brannart Morphail, with a yell, began to float upon his back, his arms waving, his feet kicking. 'It's the damned special co-ordinates every time!' he complained. He slapped the harness again and flipped over so that he was staring down at them, floating on his stomach. From the discs, the loud whizzing noise grew higher and more erratic. 'Only machine I could get working to come here. Some stupid 95th-century idea of economy! Argh!' And he was on his back again.

Mr Underwood had become very suddenly calm. He

stood regarding Brannart Morphail through his pince-nez, his face very white, his body rigid. Occasionally his lips moved.

'It's all your doing. Jherek Carnelian!' One of the discs stopped working altogether and Brannart Morphail began to drift lopsidedly across the ceiling, banging against the chandeliers and making them ring. 'You can't make these uncontrolled jaunts here and there through time without causing the most appalling eddies in the megaflow! Look what's happened now. I came to stop you, to warn you – aaah!' The scientist kicked savagely, trying to extricate himself from a velvet pelmet near the window.

In a low, unsteady voice, Mr Harris was talking to My Lady Charlotina who was stroking his head. 'All my life,' he was saying, 'I've been accused of telling tall stories. Who's going to believe this one?'

'Brannart's right, of course,' said Mr Jackson, still leaning comfortably against the pillar. 'I wonder if the risks will be worth it?'

'Risks?' said Jherek, watching as Mrs Underwood went towards her husband.

'I can't understand why the Effect has not begun to take place!' complained Brannart Morphail, floating freely again, but still unable to get the second disc working. He noticed Mr Jackson for the first time. 'What's your part in this, Lord Jagged? Something whimsical and cunning, no doubt.'

'My dear Brannart, I assure you...'

'Bah! Oof!' The disc began to whirl and the scientist was wrenched upwards and to one side. 'Neither Jherek nor that woman should still be here – nor should you, Jagged! Go against the Logic of Time and you bring doom to all!'

'Doom...' murmured Mr Underwood, unaware that his wife had reached him and was shaking his shoulder.

'Harold! Speak to me!'

He turned his head and he was smiling gently. 'Doom,' he said again. 'I should have realized. It is the Apocalypse. Do not worry, my dear, for *we* shall be saved.' He patted her hand. She burst into tears.

Mr Jackson approached Jherek who was watching this scene with anxious interest. 'I think, perhaps, it would be wise to leave now,' said Mr Jackson.

'Not without Mrs Underwood,' said Jherek firmly.

Mr Jackson sighed and shrugged. 'Of course not. Anyway, it is important that you remain together. You are so rare...'

'Rare?'

'A figure of speech.'

Mr Underwood began to sing, oblivious of his wife's tears. He sang in a surprisingly rich tenor voice. 'Jesu, lover of my soul./ Let me to thy bosom fly./ While the nearer waters roll,/ While the tempest still is high;/ Hide me, O my Saviour, hide,/ Till the storm of life is past;/ Safe into the haven guide/ O receive my soul at last.'

'How lovely!' cried the Iron Orchid. 'A primitive ritual, such as the rotted cities recall!'

'I suspect is it more of a sorcerous summoning,' said Bishop Castle, who took a special interest in such ancient customs. 'We might even say some sort of holey ghost.' He explained kindly to a rapt Donna Isobella: 'So-called because they could be seen only imperfectly. They were partly transparent, you know.'

'Aren't we all on such occasions?' said Donna Isobella. She smiled winningly at Bishop Castle who leaned over and kissed her on the lips.

'Beware!' groaned Brannart Morphail, but they had all lost interest in him. The Lat and the constables had resumed their fight.

'I must say I *like* your little century,' said the Duke of Queens to Jherek Carnelian. 'I can see why you come here.'

Jherek was flattered, in spite of his usual scepticism concerning the Duke's taste. 'Thank you, darling Duke. I didn't make it, of course.'

'You discovered it, however. I should like to come again. Is it all like this?'

'Oh, no, there's a great deal of variety.' He spoke a little vaguely, his eyes on Mr and Mrs Underwood. Mrs Underwood, still weeping, held her husband's hand and joined in the song. 'Cover my defenceless head/ With the shadow of thy wing.' Her descant was a perfect counterpart to his tenor. Jherek found himself oddly moved. He frowned. 'There's leaves, and horses, and sewage farms.'

'How do they grow sewage?'

'It's too complicated to explain.' Jherek was reluctant to admit his ignorance, particularly to his old rival.

'Perhaps, if you have a moment, you could take me on a short tour of the main features?' suggested the Duke of Queens hesitantly. 'I would be extremely grateful, Jherek.' He spoke in his most ingratiating voice and Jherek realized that, at long last, the Duke of Queens was acknowledging his superior taste. He smiled condescendingly at the Duke. 'Of course,' he said, 'when I have a moment.'

Mr Harris had fallen head down onto the table-cloth. He had begun to snore rather violently.

Jherek took a step or two towards Mrs Underwood, but then thought better of it. He did not know why he hesitated. Bishop Castle looked up. 'Join us, jaunty Jherek, please. After all, you *are* our host!'

'Not exactly,' said Jherek, but he seated himself on the other side of Donna Isobella.

The Lat had been driven into the far corner of the Café Royale, but they were putting up a spirited resistance. Not a policeman taking part in the fray was short of at least one bitten hand and bruised shin.

Jherek found himself unable to pay any attention at all to the conversation at the table. He wondered why Mrs Underwood wept so copiously as she sang. Mr Underwood's face, in contrast, was full of joy.

Donna Isobella moved a fraction closer to Jherek and he caught the mingled scents of violets and Egyptian cigarettes. Bishop Castle had begun to kiss her hand, the nails of which were painted to match her dress.

The whizzing noise from overhead grew louder again and Brannart Morphail drifted in, chest once more towards the floor. 'Get back to your own times, while you may!' he called. 'You will be stranded – marooned – abandoned! Take heed! Take hee-ee-eeeed!' And he vanished. Jherek, for one, was glad to see him go.

Donna Isobella flung back her head and flashed a bright smile at Jherek, apparently replying to something Bishop Castle had said, but addressing Jherek. 'Love love, my love,' she announced, 'but *never* commit the error of loving a person. The abstraction offers all the pleasure and nothing whatsoever of the pain. Being *in* love is so much preferable to loving *someone*.'

Jherek smiled. 'You sound a bit like Lord Jagged over there. But I'm afraid I am already trapped.'

'Besides,' said Bishop Castle, insistently keeping his hold of the lady's hand, 'who is to say which is sweeter – melancholia or mindless ecstasy?'

They both looked at him in mild astonishment.

'I have my own preferences,' she said, 'I *know*.' She returned her full attention to Jherek, saying huskily: 'But there – you are so much *younger* than I.'

'Is that so?' Jherek became interested. He had understood that, through no choice of their own, these people had extremely short life-spans. 'Well, then, you must be at least five hundred years old.'

Donna Isobella's eyes blazed. Her lip curled. She made to speak and then changed her mind. She turned her back on him. She laughed rather harshly at something Bishop Castle murmured.

He noticed, on the far side of the room, a shadowy figure whom he did not recognize. It was clad in some kind of armour, and stared about in consternation.

Lord Jagged had noticed it, too. He drew his fine brows together and puffed thoughtfully on his cigarette.

The figure disappeared almost immediately.

'Who was that, Jagged?' enquired Jherek.

'A warrior from a period six or seven centuries before this one,' said Mr Jackson. 'I can't be mistaken. And look!'

A small child, the outline of her body flickering a little, stared about her in wonderment, but was there for only a matter of seconds before she had vanished.

'Seventeenth century,' said Jagged. 'I am beginning to take Brannart's warnings seriously. The whole fabric of Time is in danger of diffusing completely. I should have been more careful. Ah, well...'

'You seem concerned, Jagged.'

'I have reason to be,' said Lord Jagged. 'You had better collect Mrs Underwood immediately.'

'She is singing, at present, with Mr Underwood.'

'So I see.'

There came a chorus of whistlings from the street and into the restaurant burst a score of uniformed policemen, their truncheons drawn. The leader presented himself to Inspector Springer and saluted. 'Sergeant Sherwood, sir.'

'In the nick of time, sergeant.' Inspector Springer rearranged his ulster and placed his battered bowler hard upon his head. 'We're cleaning up a den of forrin' anarchists 'ere, as you can observe. Are the vans outside?'

'Plenty of vans for this little lot, inspector.' Sergeant Sherwood cast a loathing eye upon the assembled company. 'I allus *knew* wot they said abart this place was true!'

'An' worse. I mean, *look* at 'em.' Inspector Springer indicated the Lat who had given up the fight and were sitting sulkily in a corner, nursing their bruises. 'You'd 'ardly believe they was yuman, would yer?'

'Ugly customers, right enough. Not English, o' course.'

'Nar! Latvians. Typical Eastern European political troublemakers. They breed 'em like that over there.'

'Wot? Special?'

'It's somefin' to do with the diet,' said Inspector

Springer. 'Curds an' so forth.'

'Oo-er. I wouldn't 'ave your job, inspector, for a million quid.'

'It *can* be nasty,' agreed Inspector Springer. 'Right. Let's get 'em all rounded up.'

'The – um – painted women, too?'

'By all means, sergeant. Every one of 'em. We'll sort out 'oo's 'oo at the Yard.'

Mr Jackson had been listening to this conversation and now he turned to Jherek with a shrug. 'I fear there is little we can do for the moment,' he said philosophically. 'We are all about to be carried off to prison.'

'Oh, really?' Jherek cheered up.

'It will be nice to be a prisoner again,' he said nostalgically. He identified gaol with one of his happiest moments, when Mr Griffiths, the lawyer, had read to him Mrs Amelia Underwood's declaration of her love. 'Perhaps they'll be able to furnish us with a time machine, too.'

Lord Jagged did not seem quite as cheerful as Jherek. 'We shall be needing one very much,' he said, 'if our problems are not to be further complicated. In more ways than one, I would say, time is running out.'

There was a sudden click and Jherek Carnelian looked down at his wrists. A newly arrived constable had snapped a pair of handcuffs on them. ''Ope you like the bracelets, sir,' said the constable with a sardonic grin.

Jherek laughed and held them up. 'Oh, they're beautiful!' he said.

In a general babble of excited merriment, the party filed out of the Café Royale and into the waiting police vans. Only Mr Harris was left behind. His snores had taken on a puzzled, melancholy note.

The Iron Orchid giggled. 'I suppose this happens to *you* all the time,' she said to Donna Isobella, whose lips seemed a little set. 'It's a rare treat for me, however.'

Mr Underwood beamed at the policemen as Mrs Underwood led him through the doors.

'Be of good cheer,' he told Inspector Springer, 'for the Lord is with us.'

Inspector Springer shook his head and sighed. 'Speak for yourself,' he said. He was not looking forward to the night ahead.

CHAPTER EIGHTEEN

TO THE TIME MACHINE, AT LAST!

'The 'Ome Secretary,' declared Inspector Springer importantly, ' 'as bin informed.' He stood with his fists upon his hips in the centre of the large cell. He looked about him at his prisoners with the self-satisfied expression of a farmer who has made a good purchase of livestock. 'I should not be surprised,' he continued, 'if we 'ave not uncovered the biggest load of conspirators against the Crown since the Gunpowder Plot. And, 'opefully, we shall in the next few days flush a few more from their foxholes.' He gave his particular attention now to Captain Mubbers and his crew. 'We shall also discover 'ow the likes o' you are smuggled inter this country.'

'Groonek, wertedas,' mumbled Captain Mubbers, staring up placatingly at Inspector Springer. 'Freg nusher, tunightly, mibix?'

'So you say, my lad! We'll let an English jury decide *your* fate!'

Captain Mubbers abandoned his attempts to reason with Inspector Springer and, with a muttered 'Kroofrudi!' retired to the company of his crew in the corner.

'We'll need a translator, inspector,' said Sergeant Sherwood, from where he stood by the door, taking down details on a clipboard. 'I couldn't get their names. All the rest,' he continued, 'seem pretty foreign, with the exception of those three.' With his pencil he indicated Mr and Mrs Underwood and the man who had given his name as 'Mr Jackson'.

'I have a pill left,' offered Jherek. 'You could take that and it would enable you to converse with them, if you were on your own...'

'Pills? You stand there and offer me, an officer of the Law, *drugs*?' He turned to Sergeant Sherwood. 'Drugs,' he said.

'That explains it.' Sergeant Sherwood nodded soberly. 'I wonder wot 'appened to that other one you mentioned. ''Im with the flying machine.'

''Is whereabouts will come to light in time,' said Inspector Springer.

'Absolutely,' said Jherek. 'I hope he got back all right. The distortion seems to have subsided, wouldn't you say, Jagged?'

'Jackson,' said Jagged, but he was not very emphatic. 'Yes, but it won't last unless we act quickly.'

Mr Underwood had stopped singing and instead was shaking his head from side to side a good deal. 'The tensions,' he was saying, 'the strain – as you say, my dear.' Mrs Underwood was soothing him. 'I apologize for my outbursts – for everything – it was un-Christian – I should have listened – if you love this man...'

'Oh, Harold!'

'No, no. I would rather you went with him. I need a rest, anyway – in the country. Perhaps I could go to stay with my sister – the one who runs the Charity House at Whitehaven. A divorce...'

'Oh, *Harold*!' She clutched his arm. 'Never. It is all right, I will stay with you.'

'What?' said Jherek. 'Don't listen to her, Mr Underwood.' But then he wished that he had not spoken. 'No, you must listen to her, I suppose...'

Mr Underwood said more firmly. 'It is not merely for your sake, Amelia. The scandal...'

'Oh, Harold. I am sorry.'

'Not your fault, I'm sure.'

'You will sue *me*?'

'Well, naturally. You could not ...'

'Harold!' This time her tears seemed to be of a different quality. 'Where would I go?'

'With – with Mr Carnelian, surely?'

'You cannot realize what that means, Harold.'

'You are used to foreign climes. If you left England, set up a new home somewhere...'

She wiped her eyes, staring accusingly at Jherek. 'This is all your doing, Mr Carnelian. Now see what has happened.'

'I can't quite see...' he began, but then gave up, for she had given her attention back to Mr Underwood.

Another policeman entered the cell. 'Aha,' said Inspector Springer. 'Sorry to get you out of bed, constable. I jest wanted to clear somefin' in my mind. You were at the execution, I believe, of the Mayfair Killer?'

'I wos, sir.'

'And would you say this chap's the one that got 'anged?' He pointed at Jherek.

'Bears a resemblance, sir. But I saw the Killer go. With a certain amount o' dignity, as wos remarked upon at the time. Couldn't be the same.'

'You saw the body – after?'

'No, sir. In fac', sir, there was a bit of a rumour went

rahnd – well ... No, sir – 'e looks sort o' different – shorter – different colour 'air an' complexion ...'

'I've changed them, since you –' began Jherek helpfully, but Inspector Springer said: 'Quiet, you!' He seemed satisfied. 'Thank you, constable.'

'Thank you, sir.' The constable left the cell.

Inspector Springer approached Mr Underwood. 'Feelin' calmer now, eh?'

'A little,' agreed Mr Underwood warily. 'I hope, I mean, you don't think I ...'

'I think you wos mistaken, that's all. 'Aving 'ad a chance ter – well – see you in different circumstances – I would say – well – that you wos a bit 'ighly-strung – not quite right in the – um –' He began again, almost kindly. 'With your missus runnin' off, an' all that. Besides, I'm grateful to yer, Mr Underwood. Not knowing, like, you 'elped me unmask this vicious gang. We've bin 'earing abaht a plan to assassinate 'Er Majesty, but the clews 'ave bin a bit thin on the ground – now we've got somefin' ter work on, see?'

'You mean, these people ...? Amelia – were you aware ...?'

'Harold!' She gestured imploringly to Jherek. 'We have told you the truth. I am sure that nobody here knows anything about such a terrible plot. They are all from the future!'

Again Inspector Springer shook his head. 'The problem will be,' he said to Sergeant Sherwood, 'in sortin' the out an' out loonies from the conscious criminals.'

The Iron Orchid yawned. 'I must say, my dear,' she murmured to Jherek, 'that you have your dull moments as well as your amusing ones in the Dawn Age.'

'It's not often like this,' he apologized.

'Therefore, sir,' said Inspector Springer to Mr Underwood, 'you can go. We'll need you as a witness, of course, but I don't think, as things stand, we want to keep you up any longer.'

'And my wife?'

'She must stay, I'm afraid.'

Mr Underwood allowed Sergeant Sherwood to lead him from the cell. 'Goodbye, my dear,' he said.

'Goodbye, Harold.' She did not seem very moved now.

The Duke of Queens drew off his magnificent hunting hat and brushed at its plumes. 'What is this stuff?' he asked Mr Jackson.

'Dust,' said Jackson. 'Grime.'

'How interesting. How do you make it?'

'There are many ways of manufacturing it in the Dawn Age,' Mr Jackson told him.

'You must tell me some of them, Jherek.' The Duke of Queens replaced his hat on his head. His voice dropped to a whisper. 'And what are we waiting for now?' he enquired eagerly.

'I am not quite sure,' Jherek said. 'But you're bound to enjoy it. I enjoy everything here.'

'Who could fail to, O banisher of boredom!' The Duke of Queens beamed benignly upon Inspector Springer. 'And I *do* love your characters, Jherek. They are in perfect key.'

Sergeant Sherwood returned with a stately-looking middle-aged man in a black tailcoat and a tall black hat. Recognizing him, Inspector Springer saluted. ''Ere they are for you, sir. I don't mind admitting it took some doing to nab 'em, but nabbed they are!'

The stately man nodded and cast a cold eye, on Lat, on Jherek, heaving a sigh. He allowed no expression to come to his face as he inspected the Iron Orchid, the Duke of Queens, Bishop Castle, My Lady Charlotina, Donna Isobella and Mrs Underwood. It was only when he took a close glance at Mr Jackson's face that he breathed a barely heard: 'Good heavens!'

'Good evening, Munroe – or is it morning, yet?' Jagged seemed amused. 'How's the Minister?'

'Is it you, Jagger?'

'I'm afraid so.'

'But, how —?'

'Ask the inspector here, my dear chap.'

'Inspector?'

'A friend of yours, sir?'

'You do not recognize Lord Charles Jagger?'

'But . . .' said Inspector Springer.

'I *told* you it was,' said Jherek in triumph to Mrs Underwood, but she silenced him.

'Did you explain anything to the inspector, Jagger?'

'It's not really his fault, but he was so convinced we were all mixed up in this business that there was no point in trying to get through to him. I thought it best to wait.'

Munroe smiled sourly. 'And got me from my bed.'

'There's the Latvians, sir,' said Inspector Springer eagerly, 'at least.'

Munroe made a stately turn and looked sternly at the Lat. 'Ah, yes. Not friends of yours, are they Jagger?'

'Not at all. Inspector Springer has done a good job there. The rest of us – all my guests – were dining at the Café Royale. As you know, I take an interest in the arts . . .'

'Of course. There is no more to be said.'

'So you're not even a bloomin' anarchist?' complained Inspector Springer moodily to Jherek. 'Just a well-connected loony.' And he uttered a deep sigh.

'Inspector!' admonished the stately gentleman.

'Sorry, sir.'

'Ferkit!' said Captain Mubbers from his corner. He seemed to be addressing Munroe. 'Gloo, mibix?'

'Ugh,' said Munroe.

None of the Lat seemed to have taken their imprisonment well. They sat in a sad little group on the floor of the cell, picking their huge noses, scratching their oddly shaped heads.

'Did you have any reason to suspect Lord Jagger and his friends, inspector?' asked Munroe distantly.

'Well, no, sir, except – well, even that wasn't . . . these green and blue women, sir –' Inspector Springer subsided. 'No, sir.'

'They have not been charged?'
'Not yet – er, no, sir.'
'They can go?'
'Yes, sir.'
'There you are, Jagger.'
'Thank you, Munroe.'
'This other business,' said Munroe, waving his stick at the disconsolate aliens, 'can wait until morning. I hope you have plenty of evidence for me, inspector.'
'Oh, yes, sir,' said Inspector Springer. In his eyes there was no light of pleasurable anticipation in the future. He stared hopelessly at the Lat. 'They're definitely forrin', sir, for a start.'
As they all entered the wide avenue of Whitehall, Lord Jagged's friend Munroe lifted his hat to the ladies. 'My compliments on your costumes,' he said. 'It must have been a marvellous ball if they were all as fine. See you at the club, perhaps, Jagger?'
'Perhaps tomorrow,' said Jagged.
Munroe made his stately way up Whitehall.
Light began to touch the tall buildings.
'Oh, look!' cried My Lady Charlotina. 'It's a proper old-fashioned dawn. A real one!'
The Duke of Queens clapped Jherek on the shoulder. 'Beautiful!'
Jherek still felt he had earned the Duke's esteem rather cheaply, considering that he had done nothing at all to produce the sun-rise, but he could not help indulging an immensely satisfying sense of identification with the wonders of the 19th century world, so again he shook his head modestly, but allowed the Duke to continue with his praise.
'Smell that air!' exclaimed the Duke of Queens. 'A thousand rich scents mingle in it! Ah!' He strode ahead of the others who followed him as he turned along the embankment, admiring the river with its flotsam, its barges, its sheen of oil, all grey in the early dawn.
Jherek said to Mrs Underwood. 'Will you now admit

that you love me, Mrs Underwood? I gather that your connection with Mr Underwood is at an end?'

'He seems to think so.' She sighed. 'I did my best.'

'Your singing was marvellous.'

'He must have been fairly unstable to begin with,' she said. 'However, I must blame myself for what happened.'

She seemed unwilling to speak further and, tactfully, Jherek shared her silence.

A tug-boat hooted from the river. Some gulls flapped upwards into a sky of soft and glowing gold, the trees lining the embankment rustled as if awakening to the new day. The others, some distance in front of Jherek and Mrs Underwood, commented on this aspect and that of the city.

'What a perfect ending to our picnic,' said the Iron Orchid to Lord Jagged. 'When shall we be going back, do you know?'

'Soon,' he said, 'I would think.'

Eventually, they left the embankment and turned into a street Jherek knew. He touched Mrs Underwood's arm. 'Do you recognize the building?'

'Yes,' she murmured, her mind evidently on other things, 'it is the Old Bailey, where they tried you.'

'Look, Jagged!' called Jherek. 'Remember?'

Lord Jagged, too, seemed abstracted. He nodded.

Laughing and chattering, the party passed the Old Bailey and paused to wonder at the next aspect of the period which had caught their fancy.

'St Paul's Cathedral,' said Donna Isobella, clinging to Bishop Castle's arm. 'Haven't you seen it before?'

'Oh, we *must* go in!'

It was then that Lord Jagged lifted his sensitive head and paused, like a fox catching wind of its hunters. He raised a hand, and Jherek and Mrs Underwood hesitated, watching as the others ran up the steps.

'A remarkable –' Bishop Castle vanished. The Iron Orchid began to laugh and then she, too, vanished. My Lady Charlotina took a step backward, and vanished.

And then the Duke of Queens, his expression amused and expectant, vanished.

Donna Isobella sat down on the steps and screamed.

They could hear Donna Isobella's screams from several streets away as Lord Jagged led them hurriedly into a maze of little cobbled alleys. 'We'll be next, if we're not lucky,' he said. 'Morphail Effect bound to manifest itself. My own fault – absolutely my own fault. Quickly...'

'Where are we going, Jagged?'

'Time machine. The one you originally came in. Repaired. Ready to go. But the fluctuations caused by recent comings and goings could have produced serious consequences. Brannart knew what he was talking about. Hurry!'

'I am not sure,' said Mrs Underwood, 'that I wish to accompany either of you. You have caused me considerable pain, you know, not to mention ...'

'Mrs Underwood,' said Lord Jagged of Canaria softly, 'you have no choice. The alternative is dreadful, I assure you.'

Convinced by his tone, she said nothing further for the moment.

They came to an alley full of bleak, festering buildings close to the river. At the far end of the alley, a few men were beginning to move boxes onto a cart. They could see the glint of the dirty Thames water.

'I feel faint,' complained Mrs Underwood. 'I cannot keep up this pace, Mr Jackson. I have had no sleep to speak of in two nights.'

'We are there,' he said. He took a key from his pocket and inserted it into the lock of a door of mouldering oak. The door creaked as he pushed it inward. Lord Jagged closed the door, reached up to take an oil lamp from a hook. He struck a match and lit the lamp.

As the light grew brighter, Jherek saw that they stood in quite a large room. The floor was stone and the whole placed smelled of mildew. He saw rats running swiftly along the beams in the roof.

Jagged had crossed to a great pile of rags and debris and began to pull them to the ground. He had lost some of his composure in his haste.

'What *is* your part in this, Mr Jackson?' said Mrs Underwood, averting her eyes from the rats. 'I am right, am I not, in believing that you have to an extent manipulated the destinies of myself and Mr Carnelian?'

'Subtly, I hope, madam,' said Jagged, still tugging at the heap. 'For so abstract a thing, Time keeps a severe eye upon our activities. I had to be careful. It is why I adopted two main disguises in this world. I have travelled in Time a great deal, as you have probably guessed. Both to the past – and the future, such as it exists at all in my world. I knew about the "End of Time" before ever Yusharisp brought the news to our planet. I also discovered that there are certain people who are, by virtue of a particular arrangement of genes, not so prone to the Morphail Effect as are others. I conceived a means of averting disaster for some of us...'

'Disaster, Jagged?'

'The end of all of us, dear Jherek. I could not bear to think that, having achieved such balance, we should perish. We had learned, you see, how to live. And it was for nothing. Such an irony was unbearable to me, the lover of ironies. I spent many, many years in this century – the furthest back I could go in my own machine – running complicated checks, taking a variety of people into the future, seeing how, as it were, they "took" when returned to their own time. None did. I regret their fate. Only Mrs Underwood stayed, apparently virtually immune to the Morphail Effect!'

'So you, sir, were my abductor!' she cried.

'I am afraid so. There!' He pulled the last of the coverings free, revealing the spherical time machine which Brannart Morphail had loaned to Jherek on his first trip to the Dawn Age.

'I am hoping,' he continued, 'that some of us will survive the End of Time. And you can help me. This time machine can be controlled. It will take you back to our own age, Jherek, where we can continue with our experiments. At least,' he added, 'it should. The instability of the megaflow at present is worrying. But we must hope. We must hope. Now, the two of you, enter the machine. There are breathing masks for both.'

'Mr Jackson,' said Mrs Underwood. 'I will not be bullied any further.' She folded her arms across her bosom. 'Neither will I allow myself to be mesmerized by your quasi-scientific lecturings!'

'I think he is right, Mrs Underwood,' said Jherek hesitantly. 'And the reason I came to find you was because you *are* prone to the Morphail Effect. At least in a time machine we stand a chance of going to an age of our choice.'

'Remember how Jherek escaped hanging,' said Lord Jagged. He had by now opened the circular outer door of the time machine. 'That was the Morphail Effect. It would have been a paradox if he had died in that particular way in this age. I knew it. That was why I lent myself to what appeared to you, Mrs Underwood, to be his destruction. There is proof of my good-will. He is not dead.'

Reluctantly, she began to move with Jherek towards the time machine. 'I shall be able to return?' she asked.

'Almost certainly. But I am hoping that you will not wish to when you have heard me out.'

'You will accompany us?'

'My own machine is not a quarter of a mile from here. I must use it, for I cannot afford to abandon it. It is a very sophisticated model. It does not even register on Brannart's instruments. As soon as you are on your way, I will go to it and follow you. I promise you, Mrs Underwood, that I am not deceiving you. I will reveal all I know upon our return to the "End of Time".'

'Very well.'

'You will not find the interior of the machine pleasant,'

Jherek told her as he helped her into the airlock. 'You must hold your breath for a moment.' They crouched together in the cylinder. He handed her a breathing mask. 'Fit this over your head, like so . . .'

He smiled as he heard her muffled complaints.

'Fear not, Mrs Underwood. Our great adventure is almost ended. Soon we shall be back in our own dear villa, with roses climbing round the door, with our pipes and our slippers and our water closets! King Darby and Queen Joan in Camelot!' The rest of his effusion was muffled, even to his own ears, by the necessity of putting on his mask as the airlock began to fill with milky fluid. Jherek wished that there had been rubber suits of the kind normally used in the machine, for the stuff felt unpleasant and was soaking rapidly through their clothes. There was a look of outraged disgust, in fact, in Mrs Underwood's eyes.

The machine filled rapidly and they drifted into the main chamber. Here certain instruments were already flashing green and red alternately, swimming about his head. They floated, unable to control their movements, in the thick liquid. As his body turned slowly, he saw that Mrs Underwood had shut her eyes. Blue and yellow lights began to flash. The liquid became increasingly cloudy.

Figures, which he could not read, began to register on the display panels. A white light throbbed and he knew that the machine was on the very brink of beginning its journey into the future. He relaxed. Happiness filled him. Soon he would be home.

The white light burned his eyes. He became dizzy. Pain began to nag at his nerves and he stopped himself from screaming, for fear that she would hear him and be troubled.

The liquid grew dark until it was the colour of blood. His senses fled him.

He woke up knowing that the journey must be over. He tried to turn himself round so that he could see if Mrs

Underwood were awake. He could feel her body resting against his leg.

But then, surprisingly, the process began again. The green lights gave way to red, to blue and to yellow. The white light shrieked. The pain increased, the liquid became dark again.

And again he fainted.

He woke up. This time he stared directly into Mrs Underwood's pale, unconscious face. He tried to reach out to take her hand and, as if this action were enough to begin it, the process started again. The green and red alternating lights, the blue and yellow lights, the blinding whiteness, the pain, the loss of his awareness. He woke up. The machine was shuddering. From somewhere there came a grating whine.

This time he screamed, in spite of himself, and he thought that Mrs Underwood was also screaming. The white light throbbed. Suddenly it was totally black. Then a green light flickered. It went out. A red light flickered and went out. Blue and yellow lights flashed.

And then Jherek Carnelian knew that Lord Jagged's fears had been realized. There had been too many attempts at once to manipulate Time – and Time was refusing further manipulation. They were adrift. They were shifting back and forth at random on the timeflow. They were as much victims of the Morphail Effect as if they had never entered the time machine. Time was taking its vengeance on those who had sought to conquer it.

Jherek's one consolation, as he fainted again, was that at least he and Mrs Underwood were together.

CHAPTER NINETEEN

IN WHICH JHEREK CARNELIAN AND MRS AMELIA UNDERWOOD DEBATE CERTAIN MORAL PROBLEMS

'Mr Carnelian! please, Mr Carnelian, try to wake up!'

'I am awake,' he groaned, but he did not open his eyes. His skin felt pleasantly warm. There was a delicious smell in his nostrils. There was silence.

'Then open your eyes, please, Mr Carnelian,' she demanded. 'I need your advice.'

He obeyed her. He blinked. 'What an extraordinarily deep blue,' he said of the sky. 'So we are back, after all. I became a trifle pessimistic, I must admit, when the machine seemed to be malfunctioning. How did we get out?'

'I pulled you out, and it was as well I did.' She made a gesture. He looked and saw that the time machine was in even worse condition than when he had landed in the 19th century. Mrs Underwood was brushing sand from her tattered dress of maroon velvet. 'That awful stuff,' she said. 'Even when it dries it makes everything stiff.'

He sat up, smiling. 'It will be the work of a moment to supply you with fresh clothes. I still have most of my power rings. I wonder who made this. It is ravishing!'

The scenery stretched for miles, all waving fern-like plants of a variety of sizes, from the small ones carpeting the ground to very large ones as big as poplars; and not far from the beach on which they lay was a lazy sea, stretching to the horizon. In the far distance behind them was a line of low, gentle hills.

'It is a remarkable reproduction,' she agreed. 'Rather better in detail than most of those made by your people.'

'You know the original?'

'I studied such things once. My father was of the modern school. He did not reject Darwin out of hand.'

'Darwin loved him?' Jherek's thoughts had returned to his favourite subject.

'Darwin was a scientist, Mr Carnelian,' she said impatiently.

'And he made a world like this?'

'No, no. It isn't anything really to do with him. A figure of speech.'

'What is a "figure of speech"?'

'I will explain that later. My point was that this landscape resembles the world at a very early age of its geological development. It is tropical and typical ferns and plants are in evidence. It is probably the Ordovician period of the Paleozoic, possibly the Silurian. If this were a perfect reproduction those seas you observe would team with edible life. There would be clams and so on, but no large beasts. Everything possible to sustain life, and nothing very much to threaten it!'

'I can't imagine who could have made it,' said Jherek. 'Unless it was Lady Voiceless. She built a series of early worlds a while ago – the Egyptian was her best.'

'Such a world as this would have flourished millions of years before Egypt,' said Mrs Underwood, becoming lyrical. 'Millions of years before Man – before the dinosaurs, even. Ah, it is paradise! You see, there are no signs at all of animal life as we know it.'

'There hasn't actually been any animal life, as such, for a good while,' said Jherek. 'Only that which we make for ourselves.'

'You aren't following me very closely, Mr Carnelian.'

'I am sorry. I will try. I want my moral education to begin as soon as possible. There are all sorts of things you can teach me.'

'I regard *that*,' she said, 'as my duty. I could not justify being here otherwise.' She smiled to herself. 'After all, I come from a long line of missionaries.'

'A new dress?' he said.

'If you please.'

He touched a power ring; the emerald.

Nothing happened.

He touched the diamond and then the amethyst. And nothing at all happened. He was puzzled. 'I have never known my power rings to fail me,' he said.

Mrs Underwood cleared her throat. 'It is becoming increasingly hot. Suppose we stroll into the shade of those ferns?'

He agreed. As they walked, he tried his power rings again, shaking his head in surprise.

'Strange. Perhaps when the time machine began to go awry ...'

'It went wrong, the time machine?'

'Yes. Plainly shifting back and forth in time at random. I had completely despaired of returning here.'

'Here?'

'Oh, dear,' he said.

'So,' she said, seating herself upon a reddish-coloured rock and staring around her at the mile upon mile of Silurian ferns, 'we could have travelled backwards, could we, Mr Carnelian?'

'I would say that we could have, yes.'

'So much for your friend Lord Jagged's assurances,' she said.

'Yes.' He sucked his lower lip. 'But he was afraid we had left things too late, if you recall.'

'He was correct.' Again she cleared her throat.

Jherek cleared his. 'If this is the age you think it is, am I to gather there are no people to be found here at all?'

'Not one. Not a primate.'

'We are at the beginning of Time?'

'For want of a better description, yes.' Her lovely fingers drummed rapidly against the rock. She did not seem pleased.

'Oh dear,' he said, 'we shall never see the Iron Orchid again!'

She brightened a little at this. 'We'll have to make the best of it, I suppose, and hope that we are rescued in due course.'

'The chances are slight, Mrs Underwood. Nobody has ever gone this far back. You heard Lord Jagged say that your age was the furthest he could reach into the past.'

She straightened her shoulders rather as she had done that time when they stood upon the bank of the river. 'We must build a hut, of course – preferably *two* huts – and we must test which of the life, such as it is, is edible. We must make a fire and keep it lit. We must see what the time machine will give us that is useable. Not much I would assume.'

'You are certain that this is the period...?'

'Mr Carnelian! Your power rings do not work. We have no other evidence. We must assume that we are marooned in the Silurian.'

'The Morphail Effect is supposed to send us into the future,' he said, 'not the past.'

'This is certainly no future we might expect from 1896, Mr Carnelian.'

'No.' A thought came to him. 'I was discussing the

possibility of the cyclic nature of Time with Brannart Morphail and Lord Jagged quite recently. Could we have plunged so far into the future that we are, as it were, at the start again?'

'Such theories cannot mean a great deal to us,' she told him, 'in our present circumstances.'

'I agree. But it would explain *why* we are in them, Mrs Underwood.'

She plucked a frond from over her head and began to fan herself, deliberately ignoring him.

He drew a deep breath of the rich Silurian (or possibly Ordovician) air. He stretched himself out luxuriously upon the ground. 'You yourself described this world as Paradise, Mrs Underwood. In what better place could two lovers find themselves?'

'Another abstract idea, Mr Carnelian? You surely do not refer to yourself and myself?'

'Oh, but I do!' he said dreamily. 'We could begin the human race all over again! A whole new cycle. This time we shall flourish *before* the dinosaurs. This is Paradise and we are Adolf and Eva! Or do I mean Alan and Edna?'

'I think you refer to Adam and Eve, Mr Carnelian. If you do, then you blaspheme and I wish to hear no more!'

'Blas-what?'

'Pheme.'

'Is that also to do with Morality?'

'I suppose it is, yes.'

'Could you explain, perhaps, a little further,' he asked enticingly.

'You offend against the Deity. It is a profanity to identify yourself with Adam in that way.'

'What about Eve?'

'Eve, too.'

'I am sorry.'

'You weren't to know.' She continued to fan herself with the frond. 'I suppose we had best start looking for food. Aren't you hungry?'

'I am hungry for your kisses,' he said romantically, and he stood up.

'Mr Carnelian!'

'Well,' he said, 'we can "marry" now, can't we? Mr Underwood said as much.'

'We are not divorced. Besides, even if I were divorced from Mr Underwood, there is no reason to assume that I should wish to give myself in marriage to you. Moreover, Mr Carnelian, there is nobody in the Silurian Age *to* marry us.' She seemed to think she had produced the final argument, but he had not really understood her.

'If we were to complete my moral education,' he said. 'Would you marry me then?'

'Perhaps – if everything else was properly settled – which seems unlikely now.'

He walked slowly back to the beach again and stared out over the sluggish sea, deep in thought. At his feet a small mollusc began to crawl through the sand. He watched it for a while and then, hearing a movement behind him, turned. She was standing there. She had made herself a hat of sorts from fern-leaves. She looked extremely pretty.

'I am sorry if I upset you, Mr Carnelian,' she said kindly. 'You are rather more direct than I have been used to, you see. I know that your manner is not deliberately offensive, that you are, in some ways, more innocent than I. But you have a way of saying the wrong thing – or sometimes the right thing in the wrong way.'

He shrugged. 'That is why I am so desperate for my moral education to begin. I love you, Mrs Amelia Underwood. Perhaps it was Lord Jagged who encouraged me to affect the emotion in the first place, but since then it has taken hold of me. I am its slave. I can console myself, of course, but I cannot stop loving you.'

'I am flattered.'

'And you have *said* that you loved me, but now you try to deny it.'

'I am still *Mrs* Underwood,' she pointed out gently.

The small mollusc began, tentatively, to crawl onto his foot. 'And I am still Jherek Carnelian,' he replied.

She noticed the mollusc. 'Aha! Perhaps this one is edible.'

As she reached down to inspect it, he stopped her with his hand on her shoulder. 'No,' he said. 'Let it go.'

She straightened up, smiling gently at him. 'We cannot afford to be sentimental, Mr Carnelian.'

His hand remained for an instant on her shoulder. The worn, stiffened velvet was beginning to grow soft again. 'We cannot afford not to be, I think.'

Her grey eyes were serious; then she laughed. 'Oh, very well. Let us wait, then, until we are *extremely* hungry.' Gaily, with her black buttoned boots kicking at the fine sand of that primordial shore, she began to stride along beside the thick and salty sea.

'All things bright and beautiful,' she sang, 'all creatures great and small./ All things wise and wonderful: / The Lord God made them all!'

There was a certain defiance in her manner, a certain spirited challenge to the inevitable, which made Jherek gasp with devotion.

'Self-denial, after all,' she called back over her shoulder, 'is good for the soul!'

'Ah!' He began to run after her and then slowed before he had caught up. He stared around him at the calm, Silurian world, struck suddenly by the freshness of it all, by the growing understanding that they really were the only two mammals on this whole planet. He looked up at the huge, golden sun and he blinked in its benign glare. He was full of wonder.

A little later, panting, sweating, laughing, he fell in beside her. He noticed that her expression was almost tender as she turned to look at him.

He offered her his arm.

After a second's hesitation, she took it.

They strolled together through the hot, Silurian afternoon.

'Now, Mrs Underwood,' he said contentedly, 'what *is* "self-denial"?'

The end of the second volume